WAR AND PEACE
BOOK EIGHT : 1811-12

By Leo Tolstoy

Double 9
BOOKS

War and Peace Book 8
by Leo Tolstoy

ISBN: 978-93-94973-93-0

Published by

DOUBLE 9 BOOKS

2/13-B, Ansari Road
Daryaganj, New Delhi - 110002
info@double9books.com
www.double9books.com
Tel. 011-40042856

Printed in India.

About the Author

L eo Tolstoy was a Russian creator known for his books War and Peace which is viewed as the best book of pragmatist fiction. Tolstoy is additionally viewed as world's best author by quite a few people. Additionally an ethical scholar and a social reformer, Tolstoy had extreme moralistic points of view. In later life, he turned into an intense Christian rebel and anarcho-conservative.

Leo Tolstoy Born in Yasnaya Polyana on September 9, 1828, He had a place with a notable honorable Russian family. He was the fourth among five offspring of Count Nikolai Ilyich Tolstoy and Countess Mariya Tolstaya, both of whom kicked the bucket passing on their youngsters to be raised by family members.

In 1844, Tolstoy was acknowledged into Kazan University. Incapable to graduate past the subsequent year, Tolstoy got back to Yasnava Polyana and afterward invested energy going among Moscow and St. Petersburg. With some functioning information on a few dialects, he turned into a multilingual. Yet again the recently observed youth pulled in Tolstoy towards drinking, visiting massage parlors and most betting which left him in weighty obligation and anguish however Tolstoy before long acknowledged he was carrying on with a brutish life and endeavored college tests with the expectation that he would acquire a situation with the public authority, yet finished yet up in Caucuses serving in the military continuing in the strides of his senior sibling.

In Year 1862, Leo Tolstoy wedded Sophia Andreevna Behrs, generally called Sonya, who was 16 years more youthful than him. The couple had thirteen youngsters, of which, five passed on at an early age. Sonya went about as Tolstoy's secretary, editor and monetary chief while he made two out of his most prominent works. Their initial wedded life was loaded up with happiness.

He started composing his show-stopper, War and Peace in 1862. The six volumes of the work were distributed somewhere in the range of 1863 and 1869. With 580 characters got from history and others made by Tolstoy, this extraordinary novel takes on investigating the hypothesis of history and the irrelevance of noted figures like Alexander and Napoleon. Anna Karenina, Tolstoy's next epic was begun in 1873 and distributed totally in 1878.

Contents

BOOK EIGHT : 1811-12

CHAPTER I

After Prince Andrew's engagement to Natásha, Pierre without any apparent cause suddenly felt it impossible to go on living as before. Firmly convinced as he was of the truths revealed to him by his benefactor, and happy as he had been in perfecting his inner man, to which he had devoted himself with such ardor—all the zest of such a life vanished after the engagement of Andrew and Natásha and the death of Joseph Alexéevich, the news of which reached him almost at the same time. Only the skeleton of life remained: his house, a brilliant wife who now enjoyed the favors of a very important personage, acquaintance with all Petersburg, and his court service with its dull formalities. And this life suddenly seemed to Pierre unexpectedly loathsome. He ceased keeping a diary, avoided the company of the Brothers, began going to the club again, drank a great deal, and came once more in touch with the bachelor sets, leading such a life that the Countess Hélène thought it necessary to speak severely to him about it. Pierre felt that she was right, and to avoid compromising her went away to Moscow.

In Moscow as soon as he entered his huge house in which the faded and fading princesses still lived, with its enormous retinue; as soon as, driving through the town, he saw the Iberian shrine with innumerable tapers burning before the golden covers of the icons, the Krémlin Square with its snow undisturbed by vehicles, the sleigh drivers and hovels of the SívtsevVrazhók, those old Moscovites who desired nothing, hurried nowhere, and were ending their days leisurely; when he saw those old Moscow ladies, the Moscow balls, and the English Club, he felt himself at home in a quiet haven. In Moscow he felt at peace, at home, warm and dirty as in an old dressing gown.

Moscow society, from the old women down to the children, received Pierre like a long-expected guest whose place was always ready awaiting him. For Moscow society Pierre was the nicest, kindest, most intellectual, merriest, and most magnanimous of cranks, a heedless, genial nobleman of the old Russian type. His purse was always empty because it was open to everyone.

Benefit performances, poor pictures, statues, benevolent societies, gypsy choirs, schools, subscription dinners, sprees, Freemasons, churches, and books—no one and nothing met with a refusal from him, and had it not been for two friends who had borrowed large sums from him and taken him under their protection, he would have given everything away. There was never a dinner or soiree at the club without him. As soon as he sank into his place on the sofa after two bottles of Margaux he was surrounded, and talking, disputing, and joking began. When there were quarrels, his kindly smile and well-timed jests reconciled the antagonists. The Masonic dinners were dull and dreary when he was not there.

When after a bachelor supper he rose with his amiable and kindly smile, yielding to the entreaties of the festive company to drive off somewhere with them, shouts of delight and triumph arose among the young men. At balls he danced if a partner was needed. Young ladies, married and unmarried, liked him because without making love to any of them, he was equally amiable to all, especially after supper. *"Il estcharmant; il n'a pas de sexe,"* * they said of him.

* "He is charming; he has no sex."

Pierre was one of those retired gentlemen-in-waiting of whom there were hundreds good-humoredly ending their days in Moscow.

How horrified he would have been seven years before, when he first arrived from abroad, had he been told that there was no need for him to seek or plan anything, that his rut had long been shaped, eternally predetermined, and that wriggle as he might, he would be what all in his position were. He could not have believed it! Had he not at one time longed with all his heart to establish a republic in Russia; then himself to be a Napoleon; then to be a philosopher; and then a strategist and the conqueror of Napoleon? Had he not seen the possibility of, and passionately desired, the regeneration of the sinful human race, and his own progress to the highest degree of perfection? Had he not established schools and hospitals and liberated his serfs?

But instead of all that—here he was, the wealthy husband of an unfaithful wife, a retired gentleman-in-waiting, fond of eating and drinking and, as he unbuttoned his waistcoat, of abusing the government a bit, a member of the Moscow English Club, and a universal favorite in Moscow society. For a long time he could not reconcile himself to the idea that he was one of those same retired Moscow gentlemen-in-waiting he had so despised seven years before.

Sometimes he consoled himself with the thought that he was only living this life temporarily; but then he was shocked by the thought of how many, like himself, had entered that life and that club temporarily, with all their teeth and hair, and had only left it when not a single tooth or hair remained.

In moments of pride, when he thought of his position it seemed to him that he was quite different and distinct from those other retired gentlemen-in-waiting he had formerly despised: they were empty, stupid, contented fellows, satisfied with their position, "while I am still discontented and want to do something for mankind. But perhaps all these comrades of mine struggled just like me and sought something new, a path in life of their own, and like me were brought by force of circumstances, society, and race—by that elemental force against which man is powerless—to the condition I am in," said he to himself in moments of humility; and after living some time in Moscow he no longer despised, but began to grow fond of, to respect, and to pity his comrades in destiny, as he pitied himself.

Pierre no longer suffered moments of despair, hypochondria, and disgust with life, but the malady that had formerly found expression in such acute attacks was driven inwards and never left him for a moment. "What for? Why? What is going on in the world?" he would ask himself in perplexity several times a day, involuntarily beginning to reflect anew on the meaning of the phenomena of life; but knowing by experience that there were no answers to these questions he made haste to turn away from them, and took up a book, or hurried off to the club or to ApollónNikoláevich's, to exchange the gossip of the town.

"Hélène, who has never cared for anything but her own body and is one of the stupidest women in the world," thought Pierre, "is regarded by people as the acme of intelligence and refinement, and they pay homage to her. Napoleon Bonaparte was despised by all as long as he was great, but now that he has become a wretched comedian the Emperor Francis wants to offer him his daughter in an illegal marriage. The Spaniards, through the Catholic clergy, offer praise to God for their victory over the French on the fourteenth of June, and the French, also through the Catholic clergy, offer praise because on that same fourteenth of June they defeated the Spaniards. My brother Masons swear by the blood that they are ready to sacrifice everything for their neighbor, but they do not give a ruble each to the collections for the poor, and they intrigue, the Astraea Lodge against the Manna Seekers, and fuss about an authentic Scotch carpet and a charter that nobody needs, and the meaning of which the very man who wrote it does not understand. We all profess the Christian law of forgiveness of injuries and love of our neighbors, the law in honor of which we have built in Moscow forty times forty churches—but yesterday a deserter was knouted to death and a minister of that same law of love and forgiveness, a priest, gave the soldier a cross to kiss before his execution." So thought Pierre, and the whole of this general deception which everyone accepts, accustomed as he was to it, astonished him each time as if it were something new. "I understand the deception and confusion," he thought, "but how am I to tell them all that I see? I have tried, and have always found that they too in the depths of their souls understand it as I do, and only try not to see it. So it appears that it must be so! But I—what is to become of me?" thought he. He had the unfortunate capacity many men, especially Russians, have of seeing and believing in the possibility of goodness and truth, but of seeing the evil and falsehood of life too clearly to be able to take a serious part in it. Every sphere of work was connected, in his eyes, with evil and deception. Whatever he tried to be, whatever he engaged in, the evil and falsehood of it repulsed him and blocked every path of activity. Yet he had to live and to find occupation. It was too dreadful to be under the burden of these insoluble problems, so he abandoned himself to any distraction in order to forget them. He frequented every kind of society, drank much, bought pictures, engaged in building, and above all—read.

He read, and read everything that came to hand. On coming home, while his valets were still taking off his things, he picked up a book and began to read. From reading he passed to sleeping, from sleeping to gossip in drawing rooms of the club, from gossip to carousals and women; from carousals back to gossip, reading, and wine. Drinking became more and more a physical and also a moral necessity. Though the doctors warned him that with his corpulence wine was dangerous for him, he drank a great deal. He was only quite at ease when having poured several glasses of wine mechanically into his large mouth he felt a pleasant warmth in his body, an amiability toward all his fellows, and a readiness to respond superficially to every idea without probing it deeply. Only after emptying a bottle or two did he feel dimly that the terribly tangled skein of life which previously had terrified him was not as dreadful as he had thought. He was always conscious of some aspect of that skein, as with a buzzing in his head after dinner or supper he chatted or listened to conversation or read. But under the influence of wine he said to himself: "It doesn't matter. I'll get it unraveled. I have a solution ready, but have no time now— I'll think it all out later on!" But the *later on* never came.

In the morning, on an empty stomach, all the old questions appeared as insoluble and terrible as ever, and Pierre hastily picked up a book, and if anyone came to see him he was glad.

Sometimes he remembered how he had heard that soldiers in war when entrenched under the enemy's fire, if they have nothing to do, try hard to find some occupation the more easily to bear the danger. To Pierre all men seemed like those soldiers, seeking refuge from life: some in ambition, some in cards, some in framing laws, some in women, some in toys, some in horses, some in politics, some in sport, some in wine, and some in governmental affairs. "Nothing is trivial, and nothing is important, it's all the same—only to save oneself from it as best one can," thought Pierre. "Only not to see *it*, that dreadful *it!*"

CHAPTER II

At the beginning of winter Prince Nicholas Bolkónski and his daughter moved to Moscow. At that time enthusiasm for the Emperor Alexander's regime had weakened and a patriotic and anti-French tendency prevailed there, and this, together with his past and his intellect and his originality, at once made Prince Nicholas Bolkónski an object of particular respect to the Moscovites and the center of the Moscow opposition to the government.

The prince had aged very much that year. He showed marked signs of senility by a tendency to fall asleep, forgetfulness of quite recent events, remembrance of remote ones, and the childish vanity with which he accepted the role of head of the Moscow opposition. In spite of this the old man inspired in all his visitors alike a feeling of respectful veneration—especially of an evening when he came in to tea in his old-fashioned coat and powdered wig and, aroused by anyone, told his abrupt stories of the past, or uttered yet more abrupt and scathing criticisms of the present. For them all, that old-fashioned house with its gigantic mirrors, pre-Revolution furniture, powdered footmen, and the stern shrewd old man (himself a relic of the past century) with his gentle daughter and the pretty Frenchwoman who were reverently devoted to him presented a majestic and agreeable spectacle. But the visitors did not reflect that besides the couple of hours during which they saw their host, there were also twenty-two hours in the day during which the private and intimate life of the house continued.

Latterly that private life had become very trying for Princess Mary. There in Moscow she was deprived of her greatest pleasures—

talks with the pilgrims and the solitude which refreshed her at Bald Hills—and she had none of the advantages and pleasures of city life. She did not go out into society; everyone knew that her father would not let her go anywhere without him, and his failing health prevented his going out himself, so that she was not invited to dinners and evening parties. She had quite abandoned the hope of getting married. She saw the coldness and malevolence with which the old prince received and dismissed the young men, possible suitors, who sometimes appeared at their house. She had no friends: during this visit to Moscow she had been disappointed in the two who had been nearest to her. Mademoiselle Bourienne, with whom she had never been able to be quite frank, had now become unpleasant to her, and for various reasons Princess Mary avoided her. Julie, with whom she had corresponded for the last five years, was in Moscow, but proved to be quite alien to her when they met. Just then Julie, who by the death of her brothers had become one of the richest heiresses in Moscow, was in the full whirl of society pleasures. She was surrounded by young men who, she fancied, had suddenly learned to appreciate her worth. Julie was at that stage in the life of a society woman when she feels that her last chance of marrying has come and that her fate must be decided now or never. On Thursdays Princess Mary remembered with a mournful smile that she now had no one to write to, since Julie—whose presence gave her no pleasure was here and they met every week. Like the old *émigré* who declined to marry the lady with whom he had spent his evenings for years, she regretted Julie's presence and having no one to write to. In Moscow Princess Mary had no one to talk to, no one to whom to confide her sorrow, and much sorrow fell to her lot just then. The time for Prince Andrew's return and marriage was approaching, but his request to her to prepare his father for it had not been carried out; in fact, it seemed as if matters were quite hopeless, for at every mention of the young Countess Rostóva the old prince (who apart from that was usually in a bad temper) lost control of himself. Another lately added sorrow arose from the lessons she gave her six year-old nephew. To her consternation she detected in herself in relation to little Nicholas some symptoms of her father's irritability. However often she told herself that she must not get irritable when teaching her nephew, almost every time that, pointer in hand, she sat down to show him the French alphabet, she so longed to pour her own knowledge quickly and easily into the child—who was already afraid that Auntie might at any moment get angry—that at his slightest inattention she trembled, became flustered and heated, raised her voice, and sometimes pulled him by the arm and put him in the corner. Having put him in the corner she would herself begin to cry over her cruel, evil nature, and little Nicholas, following her example, would sob, and without permission would leave his corner, come to her, pull her wet hands from her face, and comfort her. But what distressed the princess most of all was her father's irritability, which was always directed against her and had of late amounted to cruelty. Had he forced her to prostrate herself to the ground all night, had he beaten her or made her fetch wood or water, it would never have entered her mind to think her position hard; but this loving despot—the more cruel because he loved her and for that reason tormented himself and her—knew how not merely to hurt and humiliate her deliberately, but to show her that she was always to blame for everything. Of late he had exhibited a new trait that tormented Princess Mary more than anything else; this was his ever-increasing intimacy with Mademoiselle Bourienne. The idea that at the first moment of receiving the news of his son's intentions had occurred to him in jest—that if Andrew got married he himself would marry Bourienne—had evidently pleased him, and latterly he had persistently, and as it seemed to Princess Mary merely to offend her, shown special endearments to the companion and expressed his dissatisfaction with his daughter by demonstrations of love of Bourienne.

One day in Moscow in Princess Mary's presence (she thought her father did it purposely when she was there) the old prince kissed Mademoiselle Bourienne's hand and, drawing her to him, embraced her affectionately. Princess Mary flushed and ran out of the room. A few minutes later Mademoiselle Bourienne came into Princess Mary's room smiling and making cheerful remarks in her agreeable voice. Princess Mary hastily wiped away her tears, went resolutely up to Mademoiselle Bourienne, and evidently unconscious of what she was doing began shouting in angry haste at the Frenchwoman, her voice breaking: "It's horrible, vile, inhuman, to take advantage of the weakness..." She did not finish. "Leave my room," she exclaimed, and burst into sobs.

Next day the prince did not say a word to his daughter, but she noticed that at dinner he gave orders that Mademoiselle Bourienne should be served first. After dinner, when the footman handed coffee and from habit began with the princess, the prince suddenly grew furious, threw his stick at Philip, and instantly gave instructions to have him conscripted for the army.

"He doesn't obey... I said it twice... and he doesn't obey! She is the first person in this house; she's my best friend," cried the prince. "And if you allow yourself," he screamed in a fury, addressing Princess Mary for the first time, "to forget yourself again before her as you dared to do yesterday, I will show you who is master in this house. Go! Don't let me set eyes on you; beg her pardon!"

Princess Mary asked Mademoiselle Bourienne's pardon, and also her father's pardon for herself and for Philip the footman, who had begged for her intervention.

At such moments something like a pride of sacrifice gathered in her soul. And suddenly that father whom she had judged would look for his spectacles in her presence, fumbling near them and not seeing them, or would forget something that had just occurred, or take a false step with his failing legs and turn to see if anyone had noticed his feebleness, or, worst of all, at dinner when there were no visitors to excite him would suddenly fall asleep, letting his napkin drop and his shaking head sink over his plate. "He is old and feeble, and I dare to condemn him!" she thought at such moments, with a feeling of revulsion against herself.

CHAPTER III

In 1811 there was living in Moscow a French doctor—Métivier—who had rapidly become the fashion. He was enormously tall, handsome, amiable as Frenchmen are, and was, as all Moscow said, an extraordinarily clever doctor. He was received in the best houses not merely as a doctor, but as an equal.

Prince Nicholas had always ridiculed medicine, but latterly on Mademoiselle Bourienne's advice had allowed this doctor to visit him and had grown accustomed to him. Métivier came to see the prince about twice a week.

On December 6—St. Nicholas' Day and the prince's name day—all Moscow came to the prince's front door but he gave orders to admit no one and to invite to dinner only a small number, a list of whom he gave to Princess Mary.

Métivier, who came in the morning with his felicitations, considered it proper in his quality of doctor *de forcer la consigne*, * as he told Princess Mary, and went in to see the prince. It happened that on that morning of his name day the prince was in one of his worst moods. He had been going about the house all the morning finding fault with everyone and pretending not to understand what was said to him and not to be understood himself. Princess Mary well knew this mood of quiet absorbed querulousness, which generally culminated in a burst of rage, and she went about all that morning as though facing a cocked and loaded gun and awaited the inevitable explosion. Until the doctor's arrival the morning had passed off safely. After admitting the doctor, Princess Mary sat down with a book in the drawing room near the door through which she could hear all that passed in the study.

* To force the guard.

At first she heard only Métivier's voice, then her father's, then both voices began speaking at the same time, the door was flung open, and on the threshold appeared the handsome figure of the terrified Métivier with his shock of black hair, and the prince in his dressing gown and fez, his face distorted with fury and the pupils of his eyes rolled downwards.

"You don't understand?" shouted the prince, "but I do! French spy, slave of Buonaparte, spy, get out of my house! Be off, I tell you..." and he slammed the door.

Métivier, shrugging his shoulders, went up to Mademoiselle Bourienne who at the sound of shouting had run in from an adjoining room.

"The prince is not very well: bile and rush of blood to the head. Keep calm, I will call again tomorrow," said Métivier; and putting his fingers to his lips he hastened away.

Through the study door came the sound of slippered feet and the cry: "Spies, traitors, traitors everywhere! Not a moment's peace in my own house!"

After Métivier's departure the old prince called his daughter in, and the whole weight of his wrath fell on her. She was to blame that a spy had been admitted. Had he not told her, yes, told her to make a list, and not to admit anyone who was not on that list? Then why was that scoundrel admitted? She was the cause of it all. With her, he said, he could not have a moment's peace and could not die quietly.

"No, ma'am! We must part, we must part! Understand that, understand it! I cannot endure any more," he said, and left the room. Then, as if afraid she might find some means of consolation, he returned and trying to appear calm added: "And don't imagine I have said this in a moment of anger. I am calm. I have thought it over, and it will be carried out—we must part; so find some place for yourself...." But he could not restrain himself and with the virulence of which only one who loves is capable, evidently suffering himself, he shook his fists at her and screamed:

"If only some fool would marry her!" Then he slammed the door, sent for Mademoiselle Bourienne, and subsided into his study.

At two o'clock the six chosen guests assembled for dinner.

These guests—the famous Count Rostopchín, Prince Lopukhín with his nephew, General Chatróv an old war comrade of the prince's, and of the younger generation Pierre and BorísDrubetskóy—awaited the prince in the drawing room.

Borís, who had come to Moscow on leave a few days before, had been anxious to be presented to Prince Nicholas Bolkónski, and had contrived to ingratiate himself so well that the old prince in his case made an exception to the rule of not receiving bachelors in his house.

The prince's house did not belong to what is known as *fashionable society*, but his little circle—though not much talked about in town—was one it was more flattering to be received in than any other. Borís had realized this the week before when the commander in chief in his presence invited Rostopchín to dinner on St. Nicholas' Day, and Rostopchín had replied that he could not come:

"On that day I always go to pay my devotions to the relics of Prince Nicholas Bolkónski."

"Oh, yes, yes!" replied the commander in chief. "How is he?..."

The small group that assembled before dinner in the lofty old-fashioned drawing room with its old furniture resembled the solemn gathering of a court of justice. All were silent or talked in low tones. Prince Nicholas came in serious and taciturn. Princess Mary seemed even quieter and more diffident than usual. The guests were reluctant to address her, feeling that she was in no mood for their conversation. Count Rostopchín alone kept the conversation going, now relating the latest town news, and now the latest political gossip.

Lopukhín and the old general occasionally took part in the conversation. Prince Bolkónski listened as a presiding judge receives a report, only now and then, silently or by a brief word, showing that he took heed of what was being reported to him. The tone of the conversation was such as indicated that no one approved of what was being done in the political world. Incidents were related evidently confirming the opinion that everything was going from bad to worse, but whether telling a story or giving an opinion the speaker always stopped, or was stopped, at the point beyond which his criticism might touch the sovereign himself.

At dinner the talk turned on the latest political news: Napoleon's seizure of the Duke of Oldenburg's territory, and the Russian Note, hostile to Napoleon, which had been sent to all the European courts.

"Bonaparte treats Europe as a pirate does a captured vessel," said Count Rostopchín, repeating a phrase he had uttered several times before. "One only wonders at the long-suffering or blindness of the crowned heads. Now the Pope's turn has come and Bonaparte doesn't scruple to depose the head of the Catholic Church—yet all keep silent! Our sovereign alone has protested against the seizure of the Duke of Oldenburg's territory, and even..." Count Rostopchín paused, feeling that he had reached the limit beyond which censure was impossible.

"Other territories have been offered in exchange for the Duchy of Oldenburg," said Prince Bolkónski. "He shifts the Dukes about as I might move my serfs from Bald Hills to Boguchárovo or my Ryazán estates."

"The Duke of Oldenburg bears his misfortunes with admirable strength of character and resignation," remarked Borís, joining in respectfully.

He said this because on his journey from Petersburg he had had the honor of being presented to the Duke. Prince Bolkónski glanced at the young man as if about to say something in reply, but changed his mind, evidently considering him too young.

"I have read our protests about the Oldenburg affair and was surprised how badly the Note was worded," remarked Count Rostopchín in the casual tone of a man dealing with a subject quite familiar to him.

Pierre looked at Rostopchín with naïve astonishment, not understanding why he should be disturbed by the bad composition of the Note.

"Does it matter, Count, how the Note is worded," he asked, "so long as its substance is forcible?"

"My dear fellow, with our five hundred thousand troops it should be easy to have a good style," returned Count Rostopchín.

Pierre now understood the count's dissatisfaction with the wording of the Note.

"One would have thought quill drivers enough had sprung up," remarked the old prince. "There in Petersburg they are always writing—not notes only but even new laws. My Andrew there has written a whole volume of laws for Russia. Nowadays they are always writing!" and he laughed unnaturally.

There was a momentary pause in the conversation; the old general cleared his throat to draw attention.

"Did you hear of the last event at the review in Petersburg? The figure cut by the new French ambassador."

"Eh? Yes, I heard something: he said something awkward in His Majesty's presence."

"His Majesty drew attention to the Grenadier division and to the march past," continued the general, "and it seems the ambassador took no notice and allowed himself to reply that: 'We in France pay no attention to such trifles!' The Emperor did not condescend to reply. At the next review, they say, the Emperor did not once deign to address him."

All were silent. On this fact relating to the Emperor personally, it was impossible to pass any judgment.

"Impudent fellows!" said the prince. "You know Métivier? I turned him out of my house this morning. He was here; they admitted him in spite of my request that they should let no one in," he went on, glancing angrily at his daughter.

And he narrated his whole conversation with the French doctor and the reasons that convinced him that Métivier was a spy. Though these reasons were very insufficient and obscure, no one made any rejoinder.

After the roast, champagne was served. The guests rose to congratulate the old prince. Princess Mary, too, went round to him.

He gave her a cold, angry look and offered her his wrinkled, clean-shaven cheek to kiss. The whole expression of his face told her that he had not forgotten the morning's talk, that his decision remained in force, and only the presence of visitors hindered his speaking of it to her now.

When they went into the drawing room where coffee was served, the old men sat together.

Prince Nicholas grew more animated and expressed his views on the impending war.

He said that our wars with Bonaparte would be disastrous so long as we sought alliances with the Germans and thrust ourselves into European affairs, into which we had been drawn by the Peace of Tilsit. "We ought not to fight either for or against Austria. Our political interests are all in the East, and in regard to Bonaparte the only thing is to have an armed frontier and a firm policy, and he will never dare to cross the Russian frontier, as was the case in 1807!"

"How can we fight the French, Prince?" said Count Rostopchín. "Can we arm ourselves against our teachers and divinities? Look at our youths, look at our ladies! The French are our Gods: Paris is our Kingdom of Heaven."

He began speaking louder, evidently to be heard by everyone.

"French dresses, French ideas, French feelings! There now, you turned Métivier out by the scruff of his neck because he is a Frenchman and a scoundrel, but our ladies crawl after him on their knees. I went to a party last night, and there out of five ladies three were Roman Catholics and had the Pope's indulgence for doing woolwork on Sundays. And they themselves sit there nearly naked, like the signboards at our Public Baths if I may say so. Ah, when one looks at our young people, Prince, one would like to take Peter the Great's old cudgel out of the museum and belabor them in the Russian way till all the nonsense jumps out of them."

All were silent. The old prince looked at Rostopchín with a smile and wagged his head approvingly.

"Well, good-by, your excellency, keep well!" said Rostopchín, getting up with characteristic briskness and holding out his hand to the prince.

"Good-by, my dear fellow.... His words are music, I never tire of hearing him!" said the old prince, keeping hold of the hand and offering his cheek to be kissed.

Following Rostopchín's example the others also rose.

CHAPTER IV

Princess Mary as she sat listening to the old men's talk and faultfinding, understood nothing of what she heard; she only wondered whether the guests had all observed her father's hostile attitude toward her. She did not even notice the special attentions and amiabilities shown her during dinner by BorísDrubetskóy, who was visiting them for the third time already.

Princess Mary turned with absent-minded questioning look to Pierre, who hat in hand and with a smile on his face was the last of the guests to approach her after the old prince had gone out and they were left alone in the drawing room.

"May I stay a little longer?" he said, letting his stout body sink into an armchair beside her.

"Oh yes," she answered. "You noticed nothing?" her look asked.

Pierre was in an agreeable after-dinner mood. He looked straight before him and smiled quietly.

"Have you known that young man long, Princess?" he asked.

"Who?"

"Drubetskóy."

"No, not long...."

"Do you like him?"

"Yes, he is an agreeable young man.... Why do you ask me that?" said Princess Mary, still thinking of that morning's conversation with her father.

"Because I have noticed that when a young man comes on leave from Petersburg to Moscow it is usually with the object of marrying an heiress."

"You have observed that?" said Princess Mary.

"Yes," returned Pierre with a smile, "and this young man now manages matters so that where there is a wealthy heiress there he is too. I can read him like a book. At present he is hesitating whom to lay siege to—you or Mademoiselle Julie Karágina. He is very attentive to her."

"He visits them?"

"Yes, very often. And do you know the new way of courting?" said Pierre with an amused smile, evidently in that cheerful mood of good humored raillery for which he so often reproached himself in his diary.

"No," replied Princess Mary.

"To please Moscow girls nowadays one has to be melancholy. He is very melancholy with Mademoiselle Karágina," said Pierre.

"Really?" asked Princess Mary, looking into Pierre's kindly face and still thinking of her own sorrow. "It would be a relief," thought she, "if I ventured to confide what I am feeling to someone. I should like to tell everything to Pierre. He is kind and generous. It would be a relief. He would give me advice."

"Would you marry him?"

"Oh, my God, Count, there are moments when I would marry anybody!" she cried suddenly to her own surprise and with tears in her voice. "Ah, how bitter it is to love someone near to you and to feel that..." she went on in a trembling voice, "that you can do nothing for him but grieve him, and to know that you cannot alter this. Then there is only one thing left—to go away, but where could I go?"

"What is wrong? What is it, Princess?"

But without finishing what she was saying, Princess Mary burst into tears.

"I don't know what is the matter with me today. Don't take any notice—forget what I have said!"

Pierre's gaiety vanished completely. He anxiously questioned the princess, asked her to speak out fully and confide her grief to him; but she only repeated that she begged him to forget what she had said, that she did not remember what she had said, and that she had no trouble except the one he knew of—that Prince Andrew's marriage threatened to cause a rupture between father and son.

"Have you any news of the Rostóvs?" she asked, to change the subject. "I was told they are coming soon. I am also expecting Andrew any day. I should like them to meet here."

"And how does he now regard the matter?" asked Pierre, referring to the old prince.

Princess Mary shook her head.

"What is to be done? In a few months the year will be up. The thing is impossible. I only wish I could spare my brother the first moments. I wish they would come sooner. I hope to be friends with her. You have known them a long time," said Princess Mary. "Tell me honestly the whole truth: what sort of girl is she, and what do you think of her?—The real truth, because you know Andrew is risking so much doing this against his father's will that I should like to know...."

An undefined instinct told Pierre that these explanations, and repeated requests to be told the *whole truth*, expressed ill-will on the princess' part toward her future sister-in-law and a wish that he should disapprove of Andrew's choice; but in reply he said what he felt rather than what he thought.

"I don't know how to answer your question," he said, blushing without knowing why. "I really don't know what sort of girl she is; I can't analyze her at all. She is enchanting, but what makes her so I don't know. That is all one can say about her."

Princess Mary sighed, and the expression on her face said: "Yes, that's what I expected and feared."

"Is she clever?" she asked.

Pierre considered.

"I think not," he said, "and yet—yes. She does not deign to be clever.... Oh no, she is simply enchanting, and that is all."

Princess Mary again shook her head disapprovingly.

"Ah, I so long to like her! Tell her so if you see her before I do."

"I hear they are expected very soon," said Pierre.

Princess Mary told Pierre of her plan to become intimate with her future sister-in-law as soon as the Rostóvs arrived and to try to accustom the old prince to her.

CHAPTER V

B orís had not succeeded in making a wealthy match in Petersburg, so with the same object in view he came to Moscow. There he wavered between the two richest heiresses, Julie and Princess Mary. Though Princess Mary despite her plainness seemed to him more attractive than Julie, he, without knowing why, felt awkward about paying court to her. When they had last met on the old prince's name day, she had answered at random all his attempts to talk sentimentally, evidently not listening to what he was saying.

Julie on the contrary accepted his attentions readily, though in a manner peculiar to herself.

She was twenty-seven. After the death of her brothers she had become very wealthy. She was by now decidedly plain, but thought herself not merely as good-looking as before but even far more attractive. She was confirmed in this delusion by the fact that she had become a very wealthy heiress and also by the fact that the older she grew the less dangerous she became to men, and the more freely they could associate with her and avail themselves of her suppers, soirees, and the animated company that assembled at her house, without incurring any obligation. A man who would have been afraid ten years before of going every day to the house when there was a girl of seventeen there, for fear of compromising her and committing himself, would now go boldly every day and treat her not as a marriageable girl but as a sexless acquaintance.

That winter the Karágins' house was the most agreeable and hospitable in Moscow. In addition to the formal evening and dinner parties, a large company, chiefly of men, gathered there every day, supping at midnight and staying till three in the morning. Julie never missed a ball, a promenade, or a play. Her dresses were always of the latest fashion. But in spite of that she seemed to be disillusioned about everything and told everyone that she did not believe either in friendship or in love, or any of the joys of life, and expected peace only "yonder." She adopted the tone of one who has suffered a great disappointment, like a girl who has either lost the man she loved or been cruelly deceived by him. Though nothing of the kind had happened to her she was regarded in that light, and had even herself come to believe that she had suffered much in life. This melancholy, which did not prevent her amusing herself, did not hinder the young people who came to her house from passing the time pleasantly. Every visitor who came to the house paid his tribute to the melancholy mood of the hostess, and then amused himself with society gossip, dancing, intellectual games, and *bouts rimés*, which were in vogue at the Karágins'. Only a few of these young men, among them Borís, entered more deeply into Julie's melancholy, and with these she had prolonged conversations in private on the vanity of all worldly things, and to them she showed her albums filled with mournful sketches, maxims, and verses.

To Borís, Julie was particularly gracious: she regretted his early disillusionment with life, offered him such consolation of friendship as she who had herself suffered so much could render, and showed him her album. Borís sketched two trees in the album and wrote: "Rustic trees, your dark branches shed gloom and melancholy upon me."

On another page he drew a tomb, and wrote:

La mort estsecourable et la mort esttranquille. Ah! contre les douleurs il n'y a pas d'autreasile. *

* Death gives relief and death is peaceful. Ah! from suffering there is no other refuge.

Julie said this was charming

"There is something so enchanting in the smile of melancholy," she said to Borís, repeating word for word a passage she had copied from a book. "It is a ray of light in the darkness, a shade between sadness and despair, showing the possibility of consolation."

In reply Borís wrote these lines:

Aliment de poison d'une âme trop sensible, Toi, sans qui le bonheur me serait impossible, Tendre mélancholie, ah, viens me consoler, Viens calmer les tourments de ma sombre retraite, Et mêleune douceur secrète A cespleurs que je senscouler. *

*Poisonous nourishment of a too sensitive soul, Thou, without whom happiness would for me be impossible, Tender melancholy, ah, come to console me, Come to calm the torments of my gloomy retreat, And mingle a secret sweetness With these tears that I feel to be flowing.

For Borís, Julie played most doleful nocturnes on her harp. Borís read *Poor Liza* aloud to her, and more than once interrupted the reading because of the emotions that choked him. Meeting at large gatherings Julie and Borís looked on one another as the only souls who understood one another in a world of indifferent people.

Anna Mikháylovna, who often visited the Karágins, while playing cards with the mother made careful inquiries as to Julie's dowry (she was to have two estates in Pénza and the Nizhegórod forests). Anna Mikháylovna regarded the refined sadness that united her son to the wealthy Julie with emotion, and resignation to the Divine will.

"You are always charming and melancholy, my dear Julie," she said to the daughter. "Borís says his soul finds repose at your house. He has suffered so many disappointments and is so sensitive," said she to the mother. "Ah, my dear, I can't tell you how fond I have grown of Julie latterly," she said to her son. "But who could help loving her? She is an angelic being! Ah, Borís, Borís!"—she paused. "And how I pity her mother," she went on; "today she showed me her accounts and letters from Pénza (they have enormous estates there), and she, poor thing, has no one to help her, and they do cheat her so!"

Borís smiled almost imperceptibly while listening to his mother. He laughed blandly at her naïve diplomacy but listened to what she had to say, and sometimes questioned her carefully about the Pénza and Nizhegórod estates.

Julie had long been expecting a proposal from her melancholy adorer and was ready to accept it; but some secret feeling of repulsion for her, for her passionate desire to get married, for her artificiality, and a feeling of horror at renouncing the possibility of real love still restrained Borís. His leave was expiring. He spent every day and whole days at the Karágins', and every day on thinking the matter over told himself that he would propose tomorrow. But in Julie's presence, looking at her red face and chin (nearly always powdered), her moist eyes, and her expression of continual readiness to pass at once from melancholy to an unnatural rapture of married bliss, Borís could not utter the decisive words, though in imagination he had long regarded himself as the possessor of those Pénza and Nizhegórod estates and had apportioned the use of the income from them. Julie saw Borís' indecision, and sometimes the thought occurred to her that she was repulsive to him, but her feminine self-deception immediately supplied her with consolation, and she told herself that he was only shy from love. Her melancholy, however, began to turn to irritability, and not long before Borís' departure she formed a definite plan of action. Just as Borís' leave of absence was expiring, Anatole Kurágin made his appearance in Moscow, and of course in the Karágins' drawing room, and Julie, suddenly abandoning her melancholy, became cheerful and very attentive to Kurágin.

"My dear," said Anna Mikháylovna to her son, "I know from a reliable source that Prince Vasíli has sent his son to Moscow to get him married to Julie. I am so fond of Julie that I should be sorry for her. What do you think of it, my dear?"

The idea of being made a fool of and of having thrown away that whole month of arduous melancholy service to Julie, and of seeing all the revenue from the Pénza estates which he had already mentally apportioned and put to proper use fall into the hands of another, and especially into the hands of that idiot Anatole, pained Borís. He drove to the Karágins' with the firm intention of proposing. Julie met him in a gay, careless manner, spoke casually of how she had enjoyed yesterday's ball, and asked when he was leaving. Though Borís had come intentionally to speak of his love and therefore meant to be tender, he began speaking irritably of feminine inconstancy, of how easily women can turn from sadness to joy, and how their moods depend solely on who happens to be paying court to them. Julie was offended and replied that it was true that a woman needs variety, and the same thing over and over again would weary anyone.

"Then I should advise you..." Borís began, wishing to sting her; but at that instant the galling thought occurred to him that he might have to leave Moscow without having accomplished his aim, and have vainly wasted his efforts—which was a thing he never allowed to happen.

He checked himself in the middle of the sentence, lowered his eyes to avoid seeing her unpleasantly irritated and irresolute face, and said:

"I did not come here at all to quarrel with you. On the contrary..."

He glanced at her to make sure that he might go on. Her irritability had suddenly quite vanished, and her anxious, imploring eyes were fixed on him with greedy expectation. "I can always arrange so as not to see her often," thought Borís. "The affair has been begun and must be finished!" He blushed hotly, raised his eyes to hers, and said:

"You know my feelings for you!"

There was no need to say more: Julie's face shone with triumph and self-satisfaction; but she forced Borís to say all that is said on such occasions—that he loved her and had never loved any other woman more than her. She knew that for the Pénza estates and Nizhegórod forests she could demand this, and she received what she demanded.

The affianced couple, no longer alluding to trees that shed gloom and melancholy upon them, planned the arrangements of a splendid house in Petersburg, paid calls, and prepared everything for a brilliant wedding.

CHAPTER VI

At the end of January old Count Rostóv went to Moscow with Natásha and Sónya. The countess was still unwell and unable to travel but it was impossible to wait for her recovery. Prince Andrew was expected in Moscow any day, the trousseau had to be ordered and the estate near Moscow had to be sold, besides which the opportunity of presenting his future daughter-in-law to old Prince Bolkónski while he was in Moscow could not be missed. The Rostóvs' Moscow house had not been heated that winter and, as they had come only for a short time and the countess was not with them, the count decided to stay with MáryaDmítrievnaAkhrosímova, who had long been pressing her hospitality on them.

Late one evening the Rostóvs' four sleighs drove into MáryaDmítrievna's courtyard in the old Konyúsheny street. MáryaDmítrievna lived alone. She had already married off her daughter, and her sons were all in the service.

She held herself as erect, told everyone her opinion as candidly, loudly, and bluntly as ever, and her whole bearing seemed a reproach to others for any weakness, passion, or temptation—the possibility of which she did not admit. From early in the morning, wearing a dressing jacket, she attended to her household affairs, and then she drove out: on holy days to church and after the service to jails and prisons on affairs of which she never spoke to anyone. On ordinary days, after dressing, she received petitioners of various classes, of whom there were always some. Then she had dinner, a substantial

War and Peace

and appetizing meal at which there were always three or four guests; after dinner she played a game of boston, and at night she had the newspapers or a new book read to her while she knitted. She rarely made an exception and went out to pay visits, and then only to the most important persons in the town.

She had not yet gone to bed when the Rostóvs arrived and the pulley of the hall door squeaked from the cold as it let in the Rostóvs and their servants. MáryaDmítrievna, with her spectacles hanging down on her nose and her head flung back, stood in the hall doorway looking with a stern, grim face at the new arrivals. One might have thought she was angry with the travelers and would immediately turn them out, had she not at the same time been giving careful instructions to the servants for the accommodation of the visitors and their belongings.

"The count's things? Bring them here," she said, pointing to the portmanteaus and not greeting anyone. "The young ladies'? There to the left. Now what are you dawdling for?" she cried to the maids. "Get the samovar ready!... You've grown plumper and prettier," she remarked, drawing Natásha (whose cheeks were glowing from the cold) to her by the hood. "Foo! You *are* cold! Now take off your things, quick!" she shouted to the count who was going to kiss her hand. "You're half frozen, I'm sure! Bring some rum for tea!... *Bonjour*, Sónya dear!" she added, turning to Sónya and indicating by this French greeting her slightly contemptuous though affectionate attitude toward her.

When they came in to tea, having taken off their outdoor things and tidied themselves up after their journey, MáryaDmítrievna kissed them all in due order.

"I'm heartily glad you have come and are staying with me. It was high time," she said, giving Natásha a significant look. "The old man is here and his son's expected any day. You'll have to make his acquaintance. But we'll speak of that later on," she added, glancing at Sónya with a look that showed she did not want to speak of it in her presence. "Now listen," she said to the count. "What do you want tomorrow? Whom will you send for? Shinshín?" she crooked one of her fingers. "The sniveling Anna Mikháylovna? That's two.

She's here with her son. The son is getting married! Then Bezúkhov, eh? He is here too, with his wife. He ran away from her and she came galloping after him. He dined with me on Wednesday. As for them"—and she pointed to the girls—"tomorrow I'll take them first to the Iberian shrine of the Mother of God, and then we'll drive to the Super-Rogue's. I suppose you'll have everything new. Don't judge by me: sleeves nowadays are this size! The other day young Princess IrínaVasílevna came to see me; she was an awful sight—looked as if she had put two barrels on her arms. You know not a day passes now without some new fashion.... And what have you to do yourself?" she asked the count sternly.

"One thing has come on top of another: her rags to buy, and now a purchaser has turned up for the Moscow estate and for the house. If you will be so kind, I'll fix a time and go down to the estate just for a day, and leave my lassies with you."

"All right. All right. They'll be safe with me, as safe as in Chancery! I'll take them where they must go, scold them a bit, and pet them a bit," said MáryaDmítrievna, touching her goddaughter and favorite, Natásha, on the cheek with her large hand.

Next morning MáryaDmítrievna took the young ladies to the Iberian shrine of the Mother of God and to Madame Suppert-Roguet, who was so afraid of MáryaDmítrievna that she always let her have costumes at a loss merely to get rid of her. MáryaDmítrievna ordered almost the whole trousseau. When they got home she turned everybody out of the room except Natásha, and then called her pet to her armchair.

"Well, now we'll talk. I congratulate you on your betrothed. You've hooked a fine fellow! I am glad for your sake and I've known him since he was so high." She held her hand a couple of feet from the ground. Natásha blushed happily. "I like him and all his family. Now listen! You know that old Prince Nicholas much dislikes his son's marrying. The old fellow's crotchety! Of course Prince Andrew is not a child and can shift without him, but it's not nice to enter a family against a father's will. One wants to do it peacefully and lovingly. You're a clever girl and you'll know how to manage. Be kind, and use your wits. Then all will be well."

Natásha remained silent, from shyness MáryaDmítrievna supposed, but really because she disliked anyone interfering in what touched her love of Prince Andrew, which seemed to her so apart from all human affairs that no one could understand it. She loved and knew Prince Andrew, he loved her only, and was to come one of these days and take her. She wanted nothing more.

"You see I have known him a long time and am also fond of Mary, your future sister-in-law. 'Husbands' sisters bring up blisters,' but this one wouldn't hurt a fly. She has asked me to bring you two together. Tomorrow you'll go with your father to see her. Be very nice and affectionate to her: you're younger than she. When *he* comes, he'll find you already know his sister and father and are liked by them. Am I right or not? Won't that be best?"

"Yes, it will," Natásha answered reluctantly.

CHAPTER VII

Next day, by MáryaDmítrievna's advice, Count Rostóv took Natásha to call on Prince Nicholas Bolkónski. The count did not set out cheerfully on this visit, at heart he felt afraid. He well remembered the last interview he had had with the old prince at the time of the enrollment, when in reply to an invitation to dinner he had had to listen to an angry reprimand for not having provided his full quota of men. Natásha, on the other hand, having put on her best gown, was in the highest spirits. "They can't help liking me," she thought. "Everybody always has liked me, and I am so willing to do anything they wish, so ready to be fond of him—for being *his* father—and of her—for being *his* sister—that there is no reason for them not to like me...."

They drove up to the gloomy old house on the Vozdvízhenka and entered the vestibule.

"Well, the Lord have mercy on us!" said the count, half in jest, half in earnest; but Natásha noticed that her father was flurried on entering the anteroom and inquired timidly and softly whether the prince and princess were at home.

When they had been announced a perturbation was noticeable among the servants. The footman who had gone to announce them was stopped by another in the large hall and they whispered to one another. Then a maidservant ran into the hall and hurriedly said something, mentioning the princess. At last an old, cross looking footman came and announced to the Rostóvs that the prince was not receiving, but that the princess begged them to walk up. The first person who came to meet the visitors was Mademoiselle Bourienne.

She greeted the father and daughter with special politeness and showed them to the princess' room. The princess, looking excited and nervous, her face flushed in patches, ran in to meet the visitors, treading heavily, and vainly trying to appear cordial and at ease. From the first glance Princess Mary did not like Natásha. She thought her too fashionably dressed, frivolously gay and vain. She did not at all realize that before having seen her future sister-in-law she was prejudiced against her by involuntary envy of her beauty, youth, and happiness, as well as by jealousy of her brother's love for her. Apart from this insuperable antipathy to her, Princess Mary was agitated just then because on the Rostóvs' being announced, the old prince had shouted that he did not wish to see them, that Princess Mary might do so if she chose, but they were not to be admitted to him. She had decided to receive them, but feared lest the prince might at any moment indulge in some freak, as he seemed much upset by the Rostóvs' visit.

"There, my dear princess, I've brought you my songstress," said the count, bowing and looking round uneasily as if afraid the old prince might appear. "I am so glad you should get to know one another... very sorry the prince is still ailing," and after a few more commonplace remarks he rose. "If you'll allow me to leave my Natásha in your hands for a quarter of an hour, Princess, I'll drive round to see Anna Seménovna, it's quite near in the Dogs' Square, and then I'll come back for her."

The count had devised this diplomatic ruse (as he afterwards told his daughter) to give the future sisters-in-law an opportunity to talk to one another freely, but another motive was to avoid the danger of encountering the old prince, of whom he was afraid. He did not mention this to his daughter, but Natásha noticed her father's nervousness and anxiety and felt mortified by it. She blushed for him, grew still angrier at having blushed, and looked at the princess with a bold and defiant expression which said that she was not afraid of anybody. The princess told the count that she would be delighted, and only begged him to stay longer at Anna Seménovna's, and he departed.

Despite the uneasy glances thrown at her by Princess Mary—who wished to have a tête-à-tête with Natásha—Mademoiselle Bourienne remained in the room and persistently talked about Moscow amusements and theaters. Natásha felt offended by the hesitation she had noticed in the anteroom, by her father's nervousness, and by the unnatural manner of the princess who—she thought—was making a favor of receiving her, and so everything displeased her. She did not like Princess Mary, whom she thought very plain, affected, and dry. Natásha suddenly shrank into herself and involuntarily assumed an offhand air which alienated Princess Mary still more. After five minutes of irksome, constrained conversation, they heard the sound of slippered feet rapidly approaching. Princess Mary looked frightened.

The door opened and the old prince, in a dressing gown and a white nightcap, came in.

"Ah, madam!" he began. "Madam, Countess... Countess Rostóva, if I am not mistaken... I beg you to excuse me, to excuse me... I did not know, madam. God is my witness, I did not know you had honored us with a visit, and I came in such a costume only to see my daughter. I beg you to excuse me... God is my witness, I didn't know—" he repeated, stressing the word "God" so unnaturally and so unpleasantly that Princess Mary stood with downcast eyes not daring to look either at her father or at Natásha.

Nor did the latter, having risen and curtsied, know what to do. Mademoiselle Bourienne alone smiled agreeably.

"I beg you to excuse me, excuse me! God is my witness, I did not know," muttered the old man, and after looking Natásha over from head to foot he went out.

Mademoiselle Bourienne was the first to recover herself after this apparition and began speaking about the prince's indisposition. Natásha and Princess Mary looked at one another in silence, and the longer they did so without saying what they wanted to say, the greater grew their antipathy to one another.

When the count returned, Natásha was impolitely pleased and hastened to get away: at that moment she hated the stiff, elderly princess, who could place her in such an embarrassing position and had spent half an hour with her without once mentioning Prince Andrew. "I couldn't begin talking about him in the presence of that Frenchwoman," thought Natásha. The same thought was meanwhile tormenting Princess Mary. She knew what she ought to have said to Natásha, but she had been unable to say it because Mademoiselle Bourienne was in the way, and because, without knowing why, she felt it very difficult to speak of the marriage. When the count was already leaving the room, Princess Mary went up hurriedly to Natásha, took her by the hand, and said with a deep sigh:

"Wait, I must..."

Natásha glanced at her ironically without knowing why.

"Dear Natalie," said Princess Mary, "I want you to know that I am glad my brother has found happiness...."

She paused, feeling that she was not telling the truth. Natásha noticed this and guessed its reason.

"I think, Princess, it is not convenient to speak of that now," she said with external dignity and coldness, though she felt the tears choking her.

"What have I said and what have I done?" thought she, as soon as she was out of the room.

They waited a long time for Natásha to come to dinner that day. She sat in her room crying like a child, blowing her nose and sobbing. Sónya stood beside her, kissing her hair.

"Natásha, what is it about?" she asked. "What do they matter to you? It will all pass, Natásha."

"But if you only knew how offensive it was... as if I..."

"Don't talk about it, Natásha. It wasn't your fault so why should you mind? Kiss me," said Sónya.

Natásha raised her head and, kissing her friend on the lips, pressed her wet face against her.

"I can't tell you, I don't know. No one's to blame," said Natásha— "It's my fault. But it all hurts terribly. Oh, why doesn't he come?..."

She came in to dinner with red eyes. MáryaDmítrievna, who knew how the prince had received the Rostóvs, pretended not to notice how upset Natásha was and jested resolutely and loudly at table with the count and the other guests.

CHAPTER VIII

That evening the Rostóvs went to the Opera, for which MáryaDmítrievna had taken a box.

Natásha did not want to go, but could not refuse MáryaDmítrievna's kind offer which was intended expressly for her. When she came ready dressed into the ballroom to await her father, and looking in the large mirror there saw that she was pretty, very pretty, she felt even more sad, but it was a sweet, tender sadness.

"O God, if he were here now I would not behave as I did then, but differently. I would not be silly and afraid of things, I would simply embrace him, cling to him, and make him look at me with those searching inquiring eyes with which he has so often looked at me, and then I would make him laugh as he used to laugh. And his eyes—how I see those eyes!" thought Natásha. "And what do his father and sister matter to me? I love him alone, him, him, with that face and those eyes, with his smile, manly and yet childlike.... No, I had better not think of him; not think of him but forget him, quite forget him for the present. I can't bear this waiting and I shall cry in a minute!" and she turned away from the glass, making an effort not to cry. "And how can Sónya love Nicholas so calmly and quietly and wait so long and so patiently?" thought she, looking at Sónya, who also came in quite ready, with a fan in her hand. "No, she's altogether different. I can't!"

Natásha at that moment felt so softened and tender that it was not enough for her to love and know she was beloved, she wanted now, at once, to embrace the man she loved, to speak and hear from him words of love such as filled her heart. While she sat in the carriage beside her father, pensively watching the lights of the street lamps flickering on the frozen window, she felt still sadder and more in love, and forgot where she was going and with whom. Having fallen into the line of carriages, the Rostóvs' carriage drove up to the theater, its wheels squeaking over the snow. Natásha and Sónya, holding up their dresses, jumped out quickly. The count got out helped by the footmen, and, passing among men and women who were entering and the program sellers, they all three went along the corridor to the first row of boxes. Through the closed doors the music was already audible.

"Natásha, your hair!..." whispered Sónya.

An attendant deferentially and quickly slipped before the ladies and opened the door of their box. The music sounded louder and through the door rows of brightly lit boxes in which ladies sat with bare arms and shoulders, and noisy stalls brilliant with uniforms, glittered before their eyes. A lady entering the next box shot a glance of feminine envy at Natásha. The curtain had not yet risen and the overture was being played. Natásha, smoothing her gown, went in with Sónya and sat down, scanning the brilliant tiers of boxes opposite. A sensation she had not experienced for a long time—that of hundreds of eyes looking at her bare arms and neck—suddenly affected her both agreeably and disagreeably and called up a whole crowd of memories, desires and emotions associated with that feeling.

The two remarkably pretty girls, Natásha and Sónya, with Count Rostóv who had not been seen in Moscow for a long time, attracted general attention. Moreover, everybody knew vaguely of Natásha's engagement to Prince Andrew, and knew that the Rostóvs had lived in the country ever since, and all looked with curiosity at a fiancée who was making one of the best matches in Russia.

Natásha's looks, as everyone told her, had improved in the country, and that evening thanks to her agitation she was particularly pretty. She struck those who saw her by her fullness of life and beauty, combined with her indifference to everything about her. Her black eyes looked at the crowd without seeking anyone, and her delicate arm, bare to above the elbow, lay on the velvet edge of the box, while, evidently unconsciously, she opened and closed her hand in time to the music, crumpling her program. "Look, there's Alénina," said Sónya, "with her mother, isn't it?"

"Dear me, Michael Kirílovich has grown still stouter!" remarked the count.

"Look at our Anna Mikháylovna—what a headdress she has on!"

"The Karágins, Julie—and Borís with them. One can see at once that they're engaged...."

"Drubetskóy has proposed?"

"Oh yes, I heard it today," said Shinshín, coming into the Rostóvs' box.

Natásha looked in the direction in which her father's eyes were turned and saw Julie sitting beside her mother with a happy look on her face and a string of pearls round her thick red neck—which Natásha knew was covered with powder. Behind them, wearing a smile and leaning over with an ear to Julie's mouth, was Borís' handsome smoothly brushed head. He looked at the Rostóvs from under his brows and said something, smiling, to his betrothed.

"They are talking about us, about me and him!" thought Natásha. "And he no doubt is calming her jealousy of me. They needn't trouble themselves! If only they knew how little I am concerned about any of them."

Behind them sat Anna Mikháylovna wearing a green headdress and with a happy look of resignation to the will of God on her face. Their box was pervaded by that atmosphere of an affianced couple which Natásha knew so well and liked so much. She turned away and suddenly remembered all that had been so humiliating in her morning's visit.

"What right has he not to wish to receive me into his family? Oh, better not think of it—not till he comes back!" she told herself, and began looking at the faces, some strange and some familiar, in the stalls. In the front, in the very center, leaning back against the orchestra rail, stood Dólokhov in a Persian dress, his curly hair brushed up into a huge shock. He stood in full view of the audience, well aware that he was attracting everyone's attention, yet as much at ease as though he were in his own room. Around him thronged Moscow's most brilliant young men, whom he evidently dominated.

The count, laughing, nudged the blushing Sónya and pointed to her former adorer.

"Do you recognize him?" said he. "And where has he sprung from?" he asked, turning to Shinshín. "Didn't he vanish somewhere?"

"He did," replied Shinshín. "He was in the Caucasus and ran away from there. They say he has been acting as minister to some ruling prince in Persia, where he killed the Shah's brother. Now all the Moscow ladies are mad about him! It's 'Dólokhov the Persian' that does it! We never hear a word but Dólokhov is mentioned. They swear by him, they offer him to you as they would a dish of choice sterlet. Dólokhov and Anatole Kurágin have turned all our ladies' heads."

A tall, beautiful woman with a mass of plaited hair and much exposed plump white shoulders and neck, round which she wore a double string of large pearls, entered the adjoining box rustling her heavy silk dress and took a long time settling into her place.

Natásha involuntarily gazed at that neck, those shoulders, and pearls and coiffure, and admired the beauty of the shoulders and the pearls. While Natásha was fixing her gaze on her for the second time the lady looked round and, meeting the count's eyes, nodded to him and smiled. She was the Countess Bezúkhova, Pierre's wife, and the count, who knew everyone in society, leaned over and spoke to her.

"Have you been here long, Countess?" he inquired. "I'll call, I'll call to kiss your hand. I'm here on business and have brought my girls with me. They say Semënova acts marvelously. Count Pierre never used to forget us. Is he here?"

"Yes, he meant to look in," answered Hélène, and glanced attentively at Natásha.

Count Rostóv resumed his seat.

"Handsome, isn't she?" he whispered to Natásha.

"Wonderful!" answered Natásha. "She's a woman one could easily fall in love with."

Just then the last chords of the overture were heard and the conductor tapped with his stick. Some latecomers took their seats in the stalls, and the curtain rose.

As soon as it rose everyone in the boxes and stalls became silent, and all the men, old and young, in uniform and evening dress, and all the women with gems on their bare flesh, turned their whole attention with eager curiosity to the stage. Natásha too began to look at it.

CHAPTER IX

The floor of the stage consisted of smooth boards, at the sides was some painted cardboard representing trees, and at the back was a cloth stretched over boards. In the center of the stage sat some girls in red bodices and white skirts. One very fat girl in a white silk dress sat apart on a low bench, to the back of which a piece of green cardboard was glued. They all sang something. When they had finished their song the girl in white went up to the prompter's box and a man with tight silk trousers over his stout legs, and holding a plume and a dagger, went up to her and began singing, waving his arms about.

First the man in the tight trousers sang alone, then she sang, then they both paused while the orchestra played and the man fingered the hand of the girl in white, obviously awaiting the beat to start singing with her. They sang together and everyone in the theater began clapping and shouting, while the man and woman on the stage—who represented lovers—began smiling, spreading out their arms, and bowing.

After her life in the country, and in her present serious mood, all this seemed grotesque and amazing to Natásha. She could not follow the opera nor even listen to the music; she saw only the painted cardboard and the queerly dressed men and women who moved, spoke, and sang so strangely in that brilliant light. She knew what it was all meant to represent, but it was so pretentiously false and unnatural that she first felt ashamed for the actors and then amused at them. She looked at the faces of the audience, seeking in them the same sense of ridicule and perplexity she herself experienced, but they all seemed attentive to what was happening on the stage, and expressed delight which to Natásha seemed feigned. "I suppose it has to be like this!" she thought. She kept looking round in turn at the rows of pomaded heads in the stalls and then at the seminude women in the boxes, especially at Hélène in the next box, who—apparently quite unclothed—sat with a quiet tranquil smile, not taking her eyes off the stage. And feeling the bright light that flooded the whole place and the warm air heated by the crowd, Natásha little by little began to pass into a state of intoxication she had not experienced for a long while. She did not realize who and where she was, nor what was going on before her. As she looked and thought, the strangest fancies unexpectedly and disconnectedly passed through her mind: the idea occurred to her of jumping onto the edge of the box and singing the aria the actress was singing, then she wished to touch with her fan an old gentleman sitting not far from her, then to lean over to Hélène and tickle her.

At a moment when all was quiet before the commencement of a song, a door leading to the stalls on the side nearest the Rostóvs' box creaked, and the steps of a belated arrival were heard. "There's Kurágin!" whispered Shinshín. Countess Bezúkhova turned smiling to the newcomer, and Natásha, following the direction of that look, saw an exceptionally handsome adjutant approaching their box with a self-assured yet courteous bearing. This was Anatole Kurágin whom she had seen and noticed long ago at the ball in Petersburg. He was now in an adjutant's uniform with one epaulet and a shoulder knot. He moved with a restrained swagger which would have been ridiculous had he not been so good-looking and had his handsome face not worn such an expression of good-humored complacency and gaiety. Though the performance was proceeding, he walked deliberately down the carpeted gangway, his sword and spurs slightly jingling and his handsome perfumed head held high. Having looked at Natásha he approached his sister, laid his well gloved hand on the edge of her box, nodded to her, and leaning forward asked a question, with a motion toward Natásha.

"*Mais charmante!*" said he, evidently referring to Natásha, who did not exactly hear his words but understood them from the movement of his lips. Then he took his place in the first row of the stalls and sat down beside Dólokhov, nudging with his elbow in a friendly and offhand way that Dólokhov whom others treated so fawningly. He winked at him gaily, smiled, and rested his foot against the orchestra screen.

"How like the brother is to the sister," remarked the count. "And how handsome they both are!"

Shinshín, lowering his voice, began to tell the count of some intrigue of Kurágin's in Moscow, and Natásha tried to overhear it just because he had said she was *"charmante."*

The first act was over. In the stalls everyone began moving about, going out and coming in.

Borís came to the Rostóvs' box, received their congratulations very simply, and raising his eyebrows with an absent-minded smile conveyed to Natásha and Sónya his fiancée's invitation to her wedding, and went away. Natásha with a gay, coquettish smile talked to him, and congratulated on his approaching wedding that same Borís with whom she had formerly been in love. In the state of intoxication she was in, everything seemed simple and natural.

The scantily clad Hélène smiled at everyone in the same way, and Natásha gave Borís a similar smile.

Hélène's box was filled and surrounded from the stalls by the most distinguished and intellectual men, who seemed to vie with one another in their wish to let everyone see that they knew her.

During the whole of that entr'acte Kurágin stood with Dólokhov in front of the orchestra partition, looking at the Rostóvs' box. Natásha knew he was talking about her and this afforded her pleasure. She even turned so that he should see her profile in what she thought was its most becoming aspect. Before the beginning of the second act Pierre appeared in the stalls. The Rostóvs had not seen him since their arrival. His face looked sad, and he had grown still stouter since Natásha last saw him. He passed up to the front rows, not noticing anyone. Anatole went up to him and began speaking to him, looking at and indicating the Rostóvs' box. On seeing Natásha Pierre grew animated and, hastily passing between the rows, came toward their box. When he got there he leaned on his elbows and, smiling, talked to her for a long time. While conversing with Pierre, Natásha heard a man's voice in Countess Bezúkhova's box and something told her it was Kurágin. She turned and their eyes met. Almost smiling, he gazed straight into her eyes with such an enraptured caressing look that it seemed strange to be so near him, to look at him like that, to be so sure he admired her, and not to be acquainted with him.

In the second act there was scenery representing tombstones, there was a round hole in the canvas to represent the moon, shades were raised over the footlights, and from horns and contrabass came deep notes while many people appeared from right and left wearing black cloaks and holding things like daggers in their hands. They began waving their arms. Then some other people ran in and began dragging away the maiden who had been in white and was now in light blue. They did not drag her away at once, but sang with her for a long time and then at last dragged her off, and behind the scenes something metallic was struck three times and everyone knelt down and sang a prayer. All these things were repeatedly interrupted by the enthusiastic shouts of the audience.

During this act every time Natásha looked toward the stalls she saw Anatole Kurágin with an arm thrown across the back of his chair, staring at her. She was pleased to see that he was captivated by her and it did not occur to her that there was anything wrong in it.

When the second act was over Countess Bezúkhova rose, turned to the Rostóvs' box—her whole bosom completely exposed—beckoned the old count with a gloved finger, and paying no attention to those who had entered her box began talking to him with an amiable smile.

"Do make me acquainted with your charming daughters," said she. "The whole town is singing their praises and I don't even know them!"

Natásha rose and curtsied to the splendid countess. She was so pleased by praise from this brilliant beauty that she blushed with pleasure.

"I want to become a Moscovite too, now," said Hélène. "How is it you're not ashamed to bury such pearls in the country?"

Countess Bezúkhova quite deserved her reputation of being a fascinating woman. She could say what she did not think—especially what was flattering—quite simply and naturally.

"Dear count, you must let me look after your daughters! Though I am not staying here long this time—nor are you—I will try to amuse them. I have already heard much of you in Petersburg and wanted to get to know you," said she to Natásha with her stereotyped and lovely smile. "I had heard about you from my page, Drubetskóy. Have you heard he is getting married? And also from my husband's friend Bolkónski, Prince Andrew Bolkónski," she went on with special emphasis, implying that she knew of his relation to Natásha. To get better acquainted she asked that one of the young ladies should come into her box for the rest of the performance, and Natásha moved over to it.

The scene of the third act represented a palace in which many candles were burning and pictures of knights with short beards hung on the walls. In the middle stood what were probably a king and a queen. The king waved his right arm and, evidently nervous, sang something badly and sat down on a crimson throne. The maiden who had been first in white and then in light blue, now wore only a smock, and stood beside the throne with her hair down. She sang something mournfully, addressing the queen, but the king waved his arm severely, and men and women with bare legs came in from both sides and began dancing all together. Then the violins played very shrilly and merrily and one of the women with thick bare legs and thin arms, separating from the others, went behind the wings, adjusted her bodice, returned to the middle of the stage, and began jumping and striking one foot rapidly against the other. In the stalls everyone clapped and shouted "bravo!" Then one of the men went into a corner of the stage. The cymbals and horns in the orchestra struck up more loudly, and this man with bare legs jumped very high and waved his feet about very rapidly. (He was Duport, who received sixty thousand rubles a year for this art.) Everybody in the stalls, boxes, and galleries began clapping and shouting with all their might, and the man stopped and began smiling and bowing to all sides. Then other men and women danced with bare legs. Then the king again shouted to the sound of music, and they all began singing. But suddenly a storm came on, chromatic scales and diminished sevenths were heard in the orchestra, everyone ran off, again dragging one of their number away, and the curtain dropped. Once more there was a terrible noise and clatter among the audience, and with rapturous faces everyone began shouting: "Duport! Duport! Duport!" Natásha no longer thought this strange. She looked about with pleasure, smiling joyfully.

"Isn't Duport delightful?" Hélène asked her.

"Oh, yes," replied Natásha.

CHAPTER X

During the entr'acte a whiff of cold air came into Hélène's box, the door opened, and Anatole entered, stooping and trying not to brush against anyone.

"Let me introduce my brother to you," said Hélène, her eyes shifting uneasily from Natásha to Anatole.

Natásha turned her pretty little head toward the elegant young officer and smiled at him over her bare shoulder. Anatole, who was as handsome at close quarters as at a distance, sat down beside her and told her he had long wished to have this happiness—ever since the Naryshkins' ball in fact, at which he had had the well-remembered pleasure of seeing her. Kurágin was much more sensible and simple with women than among men. He talked boldly and naturally, and Natásha was strangely and agreeably struck by the fact that there was nothing formidable in this man about whom there was so much talk, but that on the contrary his smile was most naïve, cheerful, and good-natured.

Kurágin asked her opinion of the performance and told her how at a previous performance Semënova had fallen down on the stage.

"And do you know, Countess," he said, suddenly addressing her as an old, familiar acquaintance, "we are getting up a costume tournament; you ought to take part in it! It will be great fun. We shall all meet at the Karágins'! Please come! No! Really, eh?" said he.

While saying this he never removed his smiling eyes from her face, her neck, and her bare arms. Natásha knew for certain that he was enraptured by her. This pleased her, yet his presence made her feel constrained and oppressed. When she was not looking at him she felt that he was looking at her shoulders, and she involuntarily caught his eye so that he should look into hers rather than this. But looking into his eyes she was frightened, realizing that there was not that barrier of modesty she had always felt between herself and other men. She did not know how it was that within five minutes she had come to feel herself terribly near to this man. When she turned away she feared he might seize her from behind by her bare arm and kiss her on the neck. They spoke of most ordinary things, yet she felt that they were closer to one another than she had ever been to any man. Natásha kept turning to Hélène and to her father, as if asking what it all meant, but Hélène was engaged in conversation with a general and did not answer her look, and her father's eyes said nothing but what they always said: "Having a good time? Well, I'm glad of it!"

During one of these moments of awkward silence when Anatole's prominent eyes were gazing calmly and fixedly at her, Natásha, to break the silence, asked him how he liked Moscow. She asked the question and blushed. She felt all the time that by talking to him she was doing something improper. Anatole smiled as though to encourage her.

"At first I did not like it much, because what makes a town pleasant *cesont les jolies femmes,* * isn't that so? But now I like it very much indeed," he said, looking at her significantly. "You'll come to the costume tournament, Countess? Do come!" and putting out his hand to her bouquet and dropping his voice, he added, "You will be the prettiest there. Do come, dear countess, and give me this flower as a pledge!"

* Are the pretty women.

Natásha did not understand what he was saying any more than he did himself, but she felt that his incomprehensible words had an improper intention. She did not know what to say and turned away as if she had not heard his remark. But as soon as she had turned away she felt that he was there, behind, so close behind her.

"How is he now? Confused? Angry? Ought I to put it right?" she asked herself, and she could not refrain from turning round. She looked straight into his eyes, and his nearness, self-assurance, and the good-natured tenderness of his smile vanquished her. She smiled just as he was doing, gazing straight into his eyes. And again she felt with horror that no barrier lay between him and her.

The curtain rose again. Anatole left the box, serene and gay. Natásha went back to her father in the other box, now quite submissive to the world she found herself in. All that was going on before her now seemed quite natural, but on the other hand all her previous thoughts of her betrothed, of Princess Mary, or of life in the country did not once recur to her mind and were as if belonging to a remote past.

In the fourth act there was some sort of devil who sang waving his arm about, till the boards were withdrawn from under him and he disappeared down below. That was the only part of the fourth act that Natásha saw. She felt agitated and tormented, and the cause of this was Kurágin whom she could not help watching. As they were leaving the theater Anatole came up to them, called their carriage, and helped them in. As he was putting Natásha in he pressed her arm above the elbow. Agitated and flushed she turned round. He was looking at her with glittering eyes, smiling tenderly.

Only after she had reached home was Natásha able clearly to think over what had happened to her, and suddenly remembering Prince Andrew she was horrified, and at tea to which all had sat down after the opera, she gave a loud exclamation, flushed, and ran out of the room.

"O God! I am lost!" she said to herself. "How could I let him?" She sat for a long time hiding her flushed face in her hands trying to realize what had happened to her, but was unable either to understand what had happened or what she felt. Everything seemed dark, obscure, and terrible. There in that enormous, illuminated theater where the bare-legged Duport, in a tinsel-decorated jacket, jumped about to the music on wet boards, and young girls and old men, and the nearly naked Hélène with her proud, calm smile, rapturously cried "bravo!"—there in the presence of that Hélène it had all seemed clear and simple; but now, alone by herself, it was incomprehensible. "What is it? What was that terror I felt of him? What is this gnawing of conscience I am feeling now?" she thought.

Only to the old countess at night in bed could Natásha have told all she was feeling. She knew that Sónya with her severe and simple views would either not understand it at all or would be horrified at such a confession. So Natásha tried to solve what was torturing her by herself.

"Am I spoiled for Andrew's love or not?" she asked herself, and with soothing irony replied: "What a fool I am to ask that! What did happen to me? Nothing! I have done nothing, I didn't lead him on at all. Nobody will know and I shall never see him again," she told herself. "So it is plain that nothing has happened and there is nothing to repent of, and Andrew can love me still. But why 'still?' O God, why isn't he here?" Natásha quieted herself for a moment, but again some instinct told her that though all this was true, and though nothing had happened, yet the former purity of her love for Prince Andrew had perished. And again in imagination she went over her whole conversation with Kurágin, and again saw the face, gestures, and tender smile of that bold handsome man when he pressed her arm.

CHAPTER XI

Anatole Kurágin was staying in Moscow because his father had sent him away from Petersburg, where he had been spending twenty thousand rubles a year in cash, besides running up debts for as much more, which his creditors demanded from his father.

His father announced to him that he would now pay half his debts for the last time, but only on condition that he went to Moscow as adjutant to the commander in chief—a post his father had procured for him—and would at last try to make a good match there. He indicated to him Princess Mary and Julie Karágina.

Anatole consented and went to Moscow, where he put up at Pierre's house. Pierre received him unwillingly at first, but got used to him after a while, sometimes even accompanied him on his carousals, and gave him money under the guise of loans.

As Shinshín had remarked, from the time of his arrival Anatole had turned the heads of the Moscow ladies, especially by the fact that he slighted them and plainly preferred the gypsy girls and French actresses—with the chief of whom, Mademoiselle George, he was said to be on intimate relations. He had never missed a carousal at Danílov's or other Moscow revelers', drank whole nights through, outvying everyone else, and was at all the balls and parties of the best society. There was talk of his intrigues with some of the ladies, and he flirted with a few of them at the balls. But he did not run after the unmarried girls, especially the rich heiresses who were most of them plain. There was a special reason for this, as he had got married two years before—a fact known only to his most intimate friends. At that time while with his regiment in Poland, a Polish landowner of small means had forced him to marry his daughter. Anatole had very soon abandoned his wife and, for a payment which he agreed to send to his father-in-law, had arranged to be free to pass himself off as a bachelor.

Anatole was always content with his position, with himself, and with others. He was instinctively and thoroughly convinced that it was impossible for him to live otherwise than as he did and that he had never in his life done anything base. He was incapable of considering how his actions might affect others or what the consequences of this or that action of his might be. He was convinced that, as a duck is so made that it must live in water, so God had made him such that he must spend thirty thousand rubles a year and always occupy a prominent position in society. He believed this so firmly that others, looking at him, were persuaded of it too and did not refuse him either a leading place in society or money, which he borrowed from anyone and everyone and evidently would not repay.

He was not a gambler, at any rate he did not care about winning. He was not vain. He did not mind what people thought of him. Still less could he be accused of ambition. More than once he had vexed his father by spoiling his own career, and he laughed at distinctions of all kinds. He was not mean, and did not refuse anyone who asked of him. All he cared about was gaiety and women, and as according to his ideas there was nothing dishonorable in these tastes, and he was incapable of considering what the gratification of his tastes entailed for others, he honestly considered himself irreproachable, sincerely despised rogues and bad people, and with a tranquil conscience carried his head high.

Rakes, those male Magdalenes, have a secret feeling of innocence similar to that which female Magdalenes have, based on the same hope of forgiveness. "All will be forgiven her, for she loved much; and all will be forgiven him, for he enjoyed much."

Dólokhov, who had reappeared that year in Moscow after his exile and his Persian adventures, and was leading a life of luxury, gambling, and dissipation, associated with his old Petersburg comrade Kurágin and made use of him for his own ends.

Anatole was sincerely fond of Dólokhov for his cleverness and audacity. Dólokhov, who needed Anatole Kurágin's name, position, and connections as a bait to draw rich young men into his gambling set, made use of him and amused himself at his expense without letting the other feel it. Apart from the advantage he derived from Anatole, the very process of dominating another's will was in itself a pleasure, a habit, and a necessity to Dólokhov.

Natásha had made a strong impression on Kurágin. At supper after the opera he described to Dólokhov with the air of a connoisseur the attractions of her arms, shoulders, feet, and hair and expressed his intention of making love to her. Anatole had no notion and was incapable of considering what might come of such love-making, as he never had any notion of the outcome of any of his actions.

"She's first-rate, my dear fellow, but not for us," replied Dólokhov.

"I will tell my sister to ask her to dinner," said Anatole. "Eh?"

"You'd better wait till she's married...."

"You know, I adore little girls, they lose their heads at once," pursued Anatole.

"You have been caught once already by a 'little girl,'" said Dólokhov who knew of Kurágin's marriage. "Take care!"

"Well, that can't happen twice! Eh?" said Anatole, with a good-humored laugh.

CHAPTER XII

The day after the opera the Rostóvs went nowhere and nobody came to see them. MáryaDmítrievna talked to the count about something which they concealed from Natásha. Natásha guessed they were talking about the old prince and planning something, and this disquieted and offended her. She was expecting Prince Andrew any moment and twice that day sent a manservant to the Vozdvízhenka to ascertain whether he had come. He had not arrived. She suffered more now than during her first days in Moscow. To her impatience and pining for him were now added the unpleasant recollection of her interview with Princess Mary and the old prince, and a fear and anxiety of which she did not understand the cause. She continually fancied that either he would never come or that something would happen to her before he came. She could no longer think of him by herself calmly and continuously as she had done before. As soon as she began to think of him, the recollection of the old prince, of Princess Mary, of the theater, and of Kurágin mingled with her thoughts. The question again presented itself whether she was not guilty, whether she had not already broken faith with Prince Andrew, and again she found herself recalling to the minutest detail every word, every gesture, and every shade in the play of expression on the face of the man who had been able to arouse in her such an incomprehensible and terrifying feeling. To the family Natásha seemed livelier than usual, but she was far less tranquil and happy than before.

On Sunday morning MáryaDmítrievna invited her visitors to Mass at her parish church—the Church of the Assumption built over the graves of victims of the plague.

"I don't like those fashionable churches," she said, evidently priding herself on her independence of thought. "God is the same everywhere. We have an excellent priest, he conducts the service decently and with dignity, and the deacon is the same. What holiness is there in giving concerts in the choir? I don't like it, it's just self-indulgence!"

MáryaDmítrievna liked Sundays and knew how to keep them. Her whole house was scrubbed and cleaned on Saturdays; neither she nor the servants worked, and they all wore holiday dress and went to church. At her table there were extra dishes at dinner, and the servants had vodka and roast goose or suckling pig. But in nothing in the house was the holiday so noticeable as in MáryaDmítrievna's broad, stern face, which on that day wore an invariable look of solemn festivity.

After Mass, when they had finished their coffee in the dining room where the loose covers had been removed from the furniture, a servant announced that the carriage was ready, and MáryaDmítrievna rose with a stern air. She wore her holiday shawl, in which she paid calls, and announced that she was going to see Prince Nicholas Bolkónski to have an explanation with him about Natásha.

After she had gone, a dressmaker from Madame Suppert-Roguet waited on the Rostóvs, and Natásha, very glad of this diversion, having shut herself into a room adjoining the drawing room, occupied herself trying on the new dresses. Just as she had put on a bodice without sleeves and only tacked together, and was turning her head to see in the glass how the back fitted, she heard in the drawing room the animated sounds of her father's voice and another's—a woman's—that made her flush. It was Hélène. Natásha had not time to take off the bodice before the door opened and Countess Bezúkhova, dressed in a purple velvet gown with a high collar, came into the room beaming with good-humored amiable smiles.

"Oh, my enchantress!" she cried to the blushing Natásha. "Charming! No, this is really beyond anything, my dear count," said she to Count Rostóv who had followed her in. "How can you live in Moscow and go nowhere? No, I won't let you off! Mademoiselle George will recite at my house tonight and there'll be some people, and if you don't bring your lovely girls—who are prettier than Mademoiselle George—I won't know you! My husband is away in Tver or I would send him to fetch you. You must come. You positively must! Between eight and nine."

She nodded to the dressmaker, whom she knew and who had curtsied respectfully to her, and seated herself in an armchair beside the looking glass, draping the folds of her velvet dress picturesquely. She did not cease chattering good-naturedly and gaily, continually praising Natásha's beauty. She looked at Natásha's dresses and praised them, as well as a new dress of her own made of "metallic gauze," which she had received from Paris, and advised Natásha to have one like it.

"But anything suits you, my charmer!" she remarked.

A smile of pleasure never left Natásha's face. She felt happy and as if she were blossoming under the praise of this dear Countess Bezúkhova who had formerly seemed to her so unapproachable and important and was now so kind to her. Natásha brightened up and felt almost in love with this woman, who was so beautiful and so kind. Hélène for her part was sincerely delighted with Natásha and wished to give her a good time. Anatole had asked her to bring him and Natásha together, and she was calling on the Rostóvs for that purpose. The idea of throwing her brother and Natásha together amused her.

Though at one time, in Petersburg, she had been annoyed with Natásha for drawing Borís away, she did not think of that now, and in her own way heartily wished Natásha well. As she was leaving the Rostóvs she called her protégée aside.

"My brother dined with me yesterday—we nearly died of laughter—he ate nothing and kept sighing for you, my charmer! He is madly, quite madly, in love with you, my dear."

Natásha blushed scarlet when she heard this.

"How she blushes, how she blushes, my pretty!" said Hélène. "You must certainly come. If you love somebody, my charmer, that is not a reason to shut yourself up. Even if you are engaged, I am sure your fiancé would wish you to go into society rather than be bored to death."

"So she knows I am engaged, and she and her husband Pierre— that good Pierre—have talked and laughed about this. So it's all right." And again, under Hélène's influence, what had seemed terrible now seemed simple and natural. "And she is such a *grande dame*, so kind, and evidently likes me so much. And why not enjoy myself?" thought Natásha, gazing at Hélène with wide-open, wondering eyes.

MáryaDmítrievna came back to dinner taciturn and serious, having evidently suffered a defeat at the old prince's. She was still too agitated by the encounter to be able to talk of the affair calmly. In answer to the count's inquiries she replied that things were all right and that she would tell about it next day. On hearing of Countess Bezúkhova's visit and the invitation for that evening, MáryaDmítrievna remarked:

"I don't care to have anything to do with Bezúkhova and don't advise you to; however, if you've promised—go. It will divert your thoughts," she added, addressing Natásha.

CHAPTER XIII

Count Rostóv took the girls to Countess Bezúkhova's. There were a good many people there, but nearly all strangers to Natásha. Count Rostóv was displeased to see that the company consisted almost entirely of men and women known for the freedom of their conduct. Mademoiselle George was standing in a corner of the drawing room surrounded by young men. There were several Frenchmen present, among them Métivier who from the time Hélène reached Moscow had been an intimate in her house. The count decided not to sit down to cards or let his girls out of his sight and to get away as soon as Mademoiselle George's performance was over.

Anatole was at the door, evidently on the lookout for the Rostóvs. Immediately after greeting the count he went up to Natásha and followed her. As soon as she saw him she was seized by the same feeling she had had at the opera—gratified vanity at his admiration of her and fear at the absence of a moral barrier between them.

Hélène welcomed Natásha delightedly and was loud in admiration of her beauty and her dress. Soon after their arrival Mademoiselle George went out of the room to change her costume. In the drawing room people began arranging the chairs and taking their seats. Anatole moved a chair for Natásha and was about to sit down beside her, but the count, who never lost sight of her, took the seat himself. Anatole sat down behind her.

Mademoiselle George, with her bare, fat, dimpled arms, and a red shawl draped over one shoulder, came into the space left vacant for her, and assumed an unnatural pose. Enthusiastic whispering was audible.

Mademoiselle George looked sternly and gloomily at the audience and began reciting some French verses describing her guilty love for her son. In some places she raised her voice, in others she whispered, lifting her head triumphantly; sometimes she paused and uttered hoarse sounds, rolling her eyes.

"Adorable! divine! delicious!" was heard from every side.

Natásha looked at the fat actress, but neither saw nor heard nor understood anything of what went on before her. She only felt herself again completely borne away into this strange senseless world—so remote from her old world—a world in which it was impossible to know what was good or bad, reasonable or senseless. Behind her sat Anatole, and conscious of his proximity she experienced a frightened sense of expectancy.

After the first monologue the whole company rose and surrounded Mademoiselle George, expressing their enthusiasm.

"How beautiful she is!" Natásha remarked to her father who had also risen and was moving through the crowd toward the actress.

"I don't think so when I look at you!" said Anatole, following Natásha. He said this at a moment when she alone could hear him. "You are enchanting... from the moment I saw you I have never ceased..."

"Come, come, Natásha!" said the count, as he turned back for his daughter. "How beautiful she is!" Natásha without saying anything stepped up to her father and looked at him with surprised inquiring eyes.

After giving several recitations, Mademoiselle George left, and Countess Bezúkhova asked her visitors into the ballroom.

The count wished to go home, but Hélène entreated him not to spoil her improvised ball, and the Rostóvs stayed on. Anatole asked Natásha for a valse and as they danced he pressed her waist and hand and told her she was bewitching and that he loved her. During the *écossaise*, which she also danced with him, Anatole said nothing when they happened to be by themselves, but merely gazed at her. Natásha lifted her frightened eyes to him, but there was such confident tenderness in his affectionate look and smile that she could not, whilst looking at him, say what she had to say. She lowered her eyes.

"Don't say such things to me. I am betrothed and love another," she said rapidly.... She glanced at him.

Anatole was not upset or pained by what she had said.

"Don't speak to me of that! What can I do?" said he. "I tell you I am madly, madly, in love with you! Is it my fault that you are enchanting?... It's our turn to begin."

Natásha, animated and excited, looked about her with wide-open frightened eyes and seemed merrier than usual. She understood hardly anything that went on that evening. They danced the *écossaise* and the *Grossvater*. Her father asked her to come home, but she begged to remain. Wherever she went and whomever she was speaking to, she felt *his* eyes upon her. Later on she recalled how she had asked her father to let her go to the dressing room to rearrange her dress, that Hélène had followed her and spoken laughingly of her brother's love, and that she again met Anatole in the little sitting room. Hélène had disappeared leaving them alone, and Anatole had taken her hand and said in a tender voice:

"I cannot come to visit you but is it possible that I shall never see you? I love you madly. Can I never...?" and, blocking her path, he brought his face close to hers.

His large, glittering, masculine eyes were so close to hers that she saw nothing but them.

"Natalie?" he whispered inquiringly while she felt her hands being painfully pressed. "Natalie?"

"I don't understand. I have nothing to say," her eyes replied.

Burning lips were pressed to hers, and at the same instant she felt herself released, and Hélène's footsteps and the rustle of her dress were heard in the room. Natásha looked round at her, and then, red and trembling, threw a frightened look of inquiry at Anatole and moved toward the door.

"One word, just one, for God's sake!" cried Anatole.

She paused. She so wanted a word from him that would explain to her what had happened and to which she could find no answer.

"Natalie, just a word, only one!" he kept repeating, evidently not knowing what to say and he repeated it till Hélène came up to them.

Hélène returned with Natásha to the drawing room. The Rostóvs went away without staying for supper.

After reaching home Natásha did not sleep all night. She was tormented by the insoluble question whether she loved Anatole or Prince Andrew. She loved Prince Andrew—she remembered distinctly how deeply she loved him. But she also loved Anatole, of that there was no doubt. "Else how could all this have happened?" thought she. "If, after that, I could return his smile when saying good-by, if I was able to let it come to that, it means that I loved him from the first. It means that he is kind, noble, and splendid, and I could not help loving him. What am I to do if I love him and the other one too?" she asked herself, unable to find an answer to these terrible questions.

CHAPTER XIV

Morning came with its cares and bustle. Everyone got up and began to move about and talk, dressmakers came again. MáryaDmítrievna appeared, and they were called to breakfast. Natásha kept looking uneasily at everybody with wide-open eyes, as if wishing to intercept every glance directed toward her, and tried to appear the same as usual.

After breakfast, which was her best time, MáryaDmítrievna sat down in her armchair and called Natásha and the count to her.

"Well, friends, I have now thought the whole matter over and this is my advice," she began. "Yesterday, as you know, I went to see Prince Bolkónski. Well, I had a talk with him.... He took it into his head to begin shouting, but I am not one to be shouted down. I said what I had to say!"

"Well, and he?" asked the count.

"He? He's crazy... he did not want to listen. But what's the use of talking? As it is we have worn the poor girl out," said MáryaDmítrievna. "My advice to you is finish your business and go back home to Otrádnoe... and wait there."

"Oh, no!" exclaimed Natásha.

"Yes, go back," said MáryaDmítrievna, "and wait there. If your betrothed comes here now—there will be no avoiding a quarrel; but alone with the old man he will talk things over and then come on to you."

Count Rostóv approved of this suggestion, appreciating its reasonableness. If the old man came round it would be all the better to visit him in Moscow or at Bald Hills later on; and if not, the wedding, against his wishes, could only be arranged at Otrádnoe.

"That is perfectly true. And I am sorry I went to see him and took her," said the old count.

"No, why be sorry? Being here, you had to pay your respects. But if he won't—that's his affair," said MáryaDmítrievna, looking for something in her reticule. "Besides, the trousseau is ready, so there is nothing to wait for; and what is not ready I'll send after you. Though I don't like letting you go, it is the best way. So go, with God's blessing!"

Having found what she was looking for in the reticule she handed it to Natásha. It was a letter from Princess Mary.

"She has written to you. How she torments herself, poor thing! She's afraid you might think that she does not like you."

"But she doesn't like me," said Natásha.

"Don't talk nonsense!" cried MáryaDmítrievna.

"I shan't believe anyone, I know she doesn't like me," replied Natásha boldly as she took the letter, and her face expressed a cold and angry resolution that caused MáryaDmítrievna to look at her more intently and to frown.

"Don't answer like that, my good girl!" she said. "What I say is true! Write an answer!"

Natásha did not reply and went to her own room to read Princess Mary's letter.

Princess Mary wrote that she was in despair at the misunderstanding that had occurred between them. Whatever her father's feelings might be, she begged Natásha to believe that she could not help loving her as the one chosen by her brother, for whose happiness she was ready to sacrifice everything.

"Do not think, however," she wrote, "that my father is ill-disposed toward you. He is an invalid and an old man who must be forgiven; but he is good and magnanimous and will love her who makes his son happy." Princess Mary went on to ask Natásha to fix a time when she could see her again.

After reading the letter Natásha sat down at the writing table to answer it. "Dear Princess," she wrote in French quickly and mechanically, and then paused. What more could she write after all that had happened the evening before? "Yes, yes! All that has happened, and now all is changed," she thought as she sat with the letter she had begun before her. "Must I break off with him? Must I really? That's awful..." and to escape from these dreadful thoughts she went to Sónya and began sorting patterns with her.

After dinner Natásha went to her room and again took up Princess Mary's letter. "Can it be that it is all over?" she thought. "Can it be that all this has happened so quickly and has destroyed all that went before?" She recalled her love for Prince Andrew in all its former strength, and at the same time felt that she loved Kurágin. She vividly pictured herself as Prince Andrew's wife, and the scenes of happiness with him she had so often repeated in her imagination, and at the same time, aglow with excitement, recalled every detail of yesterday's interview with Anatole.

"Why could that not be as well?" she sometimes asked herself in complete bewilderment. "Only so could I be completely happy; but now I have to choose, and I can't be happy without either of them. Only," she thought, "to tell Prince Andrew what has happened or to hide it from him are both equally impossible. But with *that one* nothing is spoiled. But am I really to abandon forever the joy of Prince Andrew's love, in which I have lived so long?"

"Please, Miss!" whispered a maid entering the room with a mysterious air. "A man told me to give you this—" and she handed Natásha a letter.

"Only, for Christ's sake..." the girl went on, as Natásha, without thinking, mechanically broke the seal and read a love letter from Anatole, of which, without taking in a word, she understood only that it was a letter from him—from the man she loved. Yes, she loved him, or else how could that have happened which had happened? And how could she have a love letter from him in her hand?

With trembling hands Natásha held that passionate love letter which Dólokhov had composed for Anatole, and as she read it she found in it an echo of all that she herself imagined she was feeling. "Since yesterday evening my fate has been sealed; to be loved by you or to die. There is no other way for me," the letter began. Then he went on to say that he knew her parents would not give her to him—for this there were secret reasons he could reveal only to her—but that if she loved him she need only say the word *yes*, and no human power could hinder their bliss. Love would conquer all. He would steal her away and carry her off to the ends of the earth.

"Yes, yes! I love him!" thought Natásha, reading the letter for the twentieth time and finding some peculiarly deep meaning in each word of it.

That evening MáryaDmítrievna was going to the Akhárovs' and proposed to take the girls with her. Natásha, pleading a headache, remained at home.

CHAPTER XV

O n returning late in the evening Sónya went to Natásha's room, and to her surprise found her still dressed and asleep on the sofa. Open on the table, beside her lay Anatole's letter. Sónya picked it up and read it.

As she read she glanced at the sleeping Natásha, trying to find in her face an explanation of what she was reading, but did not find it. Her face was calm, gentle, and happy. Clutching her breast to keep herself from choking, Sónya, pale and trembling with fear and agitation, sat down in an armchair and burst into tears.

"How was it I noticed nothing? How could it go so far? Can she have left off loving Prince Andrew? And how could she let Kurágin go to such lengths? He is a deceiver and a villain, that's plain! What will Nicholas, dear noble Nicholas, do when he hears of it? So this is the meaning of her excited, resolute, unnatural look the day before yesterday, yesterday, and today," thought Sónya. "But it can't be that she loves him! She probably opened the letter without knowing who it was from. Probably she is offended by it. She could not do such a thing!"

Sónya wiped away her tears and went up to Natásha, again scanning her face.

"Natásha!" she said, just audibly.

Natásha awoke and saw Sónya.

"Ah, you're back?"

And with the decision and tenderness that often come at the moment of awakening, she embraced her friend, but noticing Sónya's look of embarrassment, her own face expressed confusion and suspicion.

"Sónya, you've read that letter?" she demanded.

"Yes," answered Sónya softly.

Natásha smiled rapturously.

"No, Sónya, I can't any longer!" she said. "I can't hide it from you any longer. You know, we love one another! Sónya, darling, he writes... Sónya..."

Sónya stared open-eyed at Natásha, unable to believe her ears.

"And Bolkónski?" she asked.

"Ah, Sónya, if you only knew how happy I am!" cried Natásha. "You don't know what love is...."

"But, Natásha, can *that* be all over?"

Natásha looked at Sónya with wide-open eyes as if she could not grasp the question.

"Well, then, are you refusing Prince Andrew?" said Sónya.

"Oh, you don't understand anything! Don't talk nonsense, just listen!" said Natásha, with momentary vexation.

"But I can't believe it," insisted Sónya. "I don't understand. How is it you have loved a man for a whole year and suddenly... Why, you have only seen him three times! Natásha, I don't believe you, you're joking! In three days to forget everything and so..."

"Three days?" said Natásha. "It seems to me I've loved him a hundred years. It seems to me that I have never loved anyone before. You can't understand it.... Sónya, wait a bit, sit here," and Natásha embraced and kissed her.

"I had heard that it happens like this, and you must have heard it too, but it's only now that I feel such love. It's not the same as before. As soon as I saw him I felt he was my master and I his slave, and that I could not help loving him. Yes, his slave! Whatever he orders I shall do. You don't understand that. What can I do? What can I do, Sónya?" cried Natásha with a happy yet frightened expression.

"But think what you are doing," cried Sónya. "I can't leave it like this. This secret correspondence... How could you let him go so far?" she went on, with a horror and disgust she could hardly conceal.

"I told you that I have no will," Natásha replied. "Why can't you understand? I love him!"

"Then I won't let it come to that... I shall tell!" cried Sónya, bursting into tears.

"What do you mean? For God's sake... If you tell, you are my enemy!" declared Natásha. "You want me to be miserable, you want us to be separated...."

When she saw Natásha's fright, Sónya shed tears of shame and pity for her friend.

"But what has happened between you?" she asked. "What has he said to you? Why doesn't he come to the house?"

Natásha did not answer her questions.

"For God's sake, Sónya, don't tell anyone, don't torture me," Natásha entreated. "Remember no one ought to interfere in such matters! I have confided in you...."

"But why this secrecy? Why doesn't he come to the house?" asked Sónya. "Why doesn't he openly ask for your hand? You know Prince Andrew gave you complete freedom—if it is really so; but I don't believe it! Natásha, have you considered what these *secret reasons* can be?"

Natásha looked at Sónya with astonishment. Evidently this question presented itself to her mind for the first time and she did not know how to answer it.

"I don't know what the reasons are. But there must be reasons!"

Sónya sighed and shook her head incredulously.

"If there were reasons..." she began.

But Natásha, guessing her doubts, interrupted her in alarm.

"Sónya, one can't doubt him! One can't, one can't! Don't you understand?" she cried.

"Does he love you?"

"Does he love me?" Natásha repeated with a smile of pity at her friend's lack of comprehension. "Why, you have read his letter and you have seen him."

"But if he is dishonorable?"

"*He!* dishonorable? If you only knew!" exclaimed Natásha.

"If he is an honorable man he should either declare his intentions or cease seeing you; and if you won't do this, I will. I will write to him, and I will tell Papa!" said Sónya resolutely.

"But I can't live without him!" cried Natásha.

"Natásha, I don't understand you. And what are you saying! Think of your father and of Nicholas."

"I don't want anyone, I don't love anyone but him. How dare you say he is dishonorable? Don't you know that I love him?" screamed Natásha. "Go away, Sónya! I don't want to quarrel with you, but go, for God's sake go! You see how I am suffering!" Natásha cried angrily, in a voice of despair and repressed irritation. Sónya burst into sobs and ran from the room.

Natásha went to the table and without a moment's reflection wrote that answer to Princess Mary which she had been unable to write all the morning. In this letter she said briefly that all their misunderstandings were at an end; that availing herself of the magnanimity of Prince Andrew who when he went abroad had given her her freedom, she begged Princess Mary to forget everything and forgive her if she had been to blame toward her, but that she could not be his wife. At that moment this all seemed quite easy, simple, and clear to Natásha.

On Friday the Rostóvs were to return to the country, but on Wednesday the count went with the prospective purchaser to his estate near Moscow.

On the day the count left, Sónya and Natásha were invited to a big dinner party at the Karágins', and MáryaDmítrievna took them there. At that party Natásha again met Anatole, and Sónya noticed that she spoke to him, trying not to be overheard, and that all through dinner she was more agitated than ever. When they got home Natásha was the first to begin the explanation Sónya expected.

"There, Sónya, you were talking all sorts of nonsense about him," Natásha began in a mild voice such as children use when they wish to be praised. "We have had an explanation today."

"Well, what happened? What did he say? Natásha, how glad I am you're not angry with me! Tell me everything—the whole truth. What did he say?"

Natásha became thoughtful.

"Oh, Sónya, if you knew him as I do! He said... He asked me what I had promised Bolkónski. He was glad I was free to refuse him."

Sónya sighed sorrowfully.

"But you haven't refused Bolkónski?" said she.

"Perhaps I have. Perhaps all is over between me and Bolkónski. Why do you think so badly of me?"

"I don't think anything, only I don't understand this..."

"Wait a bit, Sónya, you'll understand everything. You'll see what a man he is! Now don't think badly of me or of him. I don't think badly of anyone: I love and pity everybody. But what am I to do?"

Sónya did not succumb to the tender tone Natásha used toward her. The more emotional and ingratiating the expression of Natásha's face became, the more serious and stern grew Sónya's.

"Natásha," said she, "you asked me not to speak to you, and I haven't spoken, but now you yourself have begun. I don't trust him, Natásha. Why this secrecy?"

"Again, again!" interrupted Natásha.

"Natásha, I am afraid for you!"

"Afraid of what?"

"I am afraid you're going to your ruin," said Sónya resolutely, and was herself horrified at what she had said.

Anger again showed in Natásha's face.

"And I'll go to my ruin, I will, as soon as possible! It's not your business! It won't be you, but I, who'll suffer. Leave me alone, leave me alone! I hate you!"

"Natásha!" moaned Sónya, aghast.

"I hate you, I hate you! You're my enemy forever!" And Natásha ran out of the room.

Natásha did not speak to Sónya again and avoided her. With the same expression of agitated surprise and guilt she went about the house, taking up now one occupation, now another, and at once abandoning them.

Hard as it was for Sónya, she watched her friend and did not let her out of her sight.

The day before the count was to return, Sónya noticed that Natásha sat by the drawing room window all the morning as if expecting something and that she made a sign to an officer who drove past, whom Sónya took to be Anatole.

Sónya began watching her friend still more attentively and noticed that at dinner and all that evening Natásha was in a strange and unnatural state. She answered questions at random, began sentences she did not finish, and laughed at everything.

After tea Sónya noticed a housemaid at Natásha's door timidly waiting to let her pass. She let the girl go in, and then listening at the door learned that another letter had been delivered.

Then suddenly it became clear to Sónya that Natásha had some dreadful plan for that evening. Sónya knocked at her door. Natásha did not let her in.

"She will run away with him!" thought Sónya. "She is capable of anything. There was something particularly pathetic and resolute in her face today. She cried as she said good-by to Uncle," Sónya remembered. "Yes, that's it, she means to elope with him, but what am I to do?" thought she, recalling all the signs that clearly indicated that Natásha had some terrible intention. "The count is away. What am I to do? Write to Kurágin demanding an explanation? But what is there to oblige him to reply? Write to Pierre, as Prince Andrew asked me to in case of some misfortune?... But perhaps she really has already refused Bolkónski—she sent a letter to Princess Mary yesterday. And Uncle is away...." To tell MáryaDmítrievna who had such faith in Natásha seemed to Sónya terrible. "Well, anyway," thought Sónya as she stood in the dark passage, "now or never I must prove that I remember the family's goodness to me and that I love Nicholas. Yes! If I don't sleep for three nights I'll not leave this passage and will hold her back by force and will and not let the family be disgraced," thought she.

CHAPTER XVI

Anatole had lately moved to Dólokhov's. The plan for Natalie Rostóva's abduction had been arranged and the preparations made by Dólokhov a few days before, and on the day that Sónya, after listening at Natásha's door, resolved to safeguard her, it was to have been put into execution. Natásha had promised to come out to Kurágin at the back porch at ten that evening. Kurágin was to put her into a troyka he would have ready and to drive her forty miles to the village of Kámenka, where an unfrocked priest was in readiness to perform a marriage ceremony over them. At Kámenka a relay of horses was to wait which would take them to the Warsaw highroad, and from there they would hasten abroad with post horses.

Anatole had a passport, an order for post horses, ten thousand rubles he had taken from his sister and another ten thousand borrowed with Dólokhov's help.

Two witnesses for the mock marriage—Khvóstikov, a retired petty official whom Dólokhov made use of in his gambling transactions, and Makárin, a retired hussar, a kindly, weak fellow who had an unbounded affection for Kurágin—were sitting at tea in Dólokhov's front room.

In his large study, the walls of which were hung to the ceiling with Persian rugs, bearskins, and weapons, sat Dólokhov in a traveling cloak and high boots, at an open desk on which lay an abacus and some bundles of paper money. Anatole, with uniform unbuttoned, walked to and fro from the room where the witnesses were sitting, through the study to the room behind, where his French valet and others were packing the last of his things. Dólokhov was counting the money and noting something down.

"Well," he said, "Khvóstikov must have two thousand."

"Give it to him, then," said Anatole.

"Makárka" (their name for Makárin) "will go through fire and water for you for nothing. So here are our accounts all settled," said Dólokhov, showing him the memorandum. "Is that right?"

"Yes, of course," returned Anatole, evidently not listening to Dólokhov and looking straight before him with a smile that did not leave his face.

Dólokhov banged down the lid of his desk and turned to Anatole with an ironic smile:

"Do you know? You'd really better drop it all. There's still time!"

"Fool," retorted Anatole. "Don't talk nonsense! If you only knew... it's the devil knows what!"

"No, really, give it up!" said Dólokhov. "I am speaking seriously. It's no joke, this plot you've hatched."

"What, teasing again? Go to the devil! Eh?" said Anatole, making a grimace. "Really it's no time for your stupid jokes," and he left the room.

Dólokhov smiled contemptuously and condescendingly when Anatole had gone out.

"You wait a bit," he called after him. "I'm not joking, I'm talking sense. Come here, come here!"

Anatole returned and looked at Dólokhov, trying to give him his attention and evidently submitting to him involuntarily.

"Now listen to me. I'm telling you this for the last time. Why should I joke about it? Did I hinder you? Who arranged everything for you? Who found the priest and got the passport? Who raised the money? I did it all."

"Well, thank you for it. Do you think I am not grateful?" And Anatole sighed and embraced Dólokhov.

"I helped you, but all the same I must tell you the truth; it is a dangerous business, and if you think about it—a stupid business. Well, you'll carry her off—all right! Will they let it stop at that? It will come out that you're already married. Why, they'll have you in the criminal court...."

"Oh, nonsense, nonsense!" Anatole ejaculated and again made a grimace. "Didn't I explain to you? What?" And Anatole, with the partiality dull-witted people have for any conclusion they have reached by their own reasoning, repeated the argument he had already put to Dólokhov a hundred times. "Didn't I explain to you that I have come to this conclusion: if this marriage is invalid," he went on, crooking one finger, "then I have nothing to answer for; but if it is valid, no matter! Abroad no one will know anything about it. Isn't that so? And don't talk to me, don't, don't."

"Seriously, you'd better drop it! You'll only get yourself into a mess!"

"Go to the devil!" cried Anatole and, clutching his hair, left the room, but returned at once and dropped into an armchair in front of Dólokhov with his feet turned under him. "It's the very devil! What? Feel how it beats!" He took Dólokhov's hand and put it on his heart. "What a foot, my dear fellow! What a glance! A goddess!" he added in French. "What?"

Dólokhov with a cold smile and a gleam in his handsome insolent eyes looked at him—evidently wishing to get some more amusement out of him.

"Well and when the money's gone, what then?"

"What then? Eh?" repeated Anatole, sincerely perplexed by a thought of the future. "What then?... Then, I don't know.... But why talk nonsense!" He glanced at his watch. "It's time!"

Anatole went into the back room.

"Now then! Nearly ready? You're dawdling!" he shouted to the servants.

Dólokhov put away the money, called a footman whom he ordered to bring something for them to eat and drink before the journey, and went into the room where Khvóstikov and Makárin were sitting.

Anatole lay on the sofa in the study leaning on his elbow and smiling pensively, while his handsome lips muttered tenderly to himself.

"Come and eat something. Have a drink!" Dólokhov shouted to him from the other room.

"I don't want to," answered Anatole continuing to smile.

"Come! Balagá is here."

Anatole rose and went into the dining room. Balagá was a famous troyka driver who had known Dólokhov and Anatole some six years and had given them good service with his troykas. More than once when Anatole's regiment was stationed at Tver he had taken him from Tver in the evening, brought him to Moscow by daybreak, and driven him back again the next night. More than once he had enabled Dólokhov to escape when pursued. More than once he had driven them through the town with gypsies and "ladykins" as he called the cocottes. More than once in their service he had run over pedestrians and upset vehicles in the streets of Moscow and had always been protected from the consequences by "my gentlemen" as he called them. He had ruined more than one horse in their service. More than once they had beaten him, and more than once they had made him drunk on champagne and Madeira, which he loved; and he knew more than one thing about each of them which would long ago have sent an ordinary man to Siberia. They often called Balagá into their orgies and made him drink and dance at the gypsies', and more than one thousand rubles of their money had passed through his hands. In their service he risked his skin and his life twenty times a year, and in their service had lost more horses than the money he had from them would buy. But he liked them; liked that mad driving at twelve miles an hour, liked upsetting a driver or running down a pedestrian, and flying at full gallop through the Moscow streets. He liked to hear those wild, tipsy shouts behind him: "Get on! Get on!" when it was impossible to go any faster. He liked giving a painful lash on the neck to some peasant who, more dead than alive, was already hurrying out of his way. "Real gentlemen!" he considered them.

Anatole and Dólokhov liked Balagá too for his masterly driving and because he liked the things they liked. With others Balagá bargained, charging twenty-five rubles for a two hours' drive, and rarely drove himself, generally letting his young men do so. But with "his gentlemen" he always drove himself and never demanded anything for his work. Only a couple of times a year—when he knew from their valets that they had money in hand—he would turn up of a morning quite sober and with a deep bow would ask them to help him. The gentlemen always made him sit down.

"Do help me out, Theodore Iványch, sir," or "your excellency," he would say. "I am quite out of horses. Let me have what you can to go to the fair."

And Anatole and Dólokhov, when they had money, would give him a thousand or a couple of thousand rubles.

Balagá was a fair-haired, short, and snub-nosed peasant of about twenty-seven; red-faced, with a particularly red thick neck, glittering little eyes, and a small beard. He wore a fine, dark-blue, silk-lined cloth coat over a sheepskin.

On entering the room now he crossed himself, turning toward the front corner of the room, and went up to Dólokhov, holding out a small, black hand.

"Theodore Iványch!" he said, bowing.

"How d'you do, friend? Well, here he is!"

"Good day, your excellency!" he said, again holding out his hand to Anatole who had just come in.

"I say, Balagá," said Anatole, putting his hands on the man's shoulders, "do you care for me or not? Eh? Now, do me a service.... What horses have you come with? Eh?"

"As your messenger ordered, your special beasts," replied Balagá.

"Well, listen, Balagá! Drive all three to death but get me there in three hours. Eh?"

"When they are dead, what shall I drive?" said Balagá with a wink.

"Mind, I'll smash your face in! Don't make jokes!" cried Anatole, suddenly rolling his eyes.

"Why joke?" said the driver, laughing. "As if I'd grudge my gentlemen anything! As fast as ever the horses can gallop, so fast we'll go!"

"Ah!" said Anatole. "Well, sit down."

"Yes, sit down!" said Dólokhov.

"I'll stand, Theodore Iványch."

"Sit down; nonsense! Have a drink!" said Anatole, and filled a large glass of Madeira for him.

The driver's eyes sparkled at the sight of the wine. After refusing it for manners' sake, he drank it and wiped his mouth with a red silk handkerchief he took out of his cap.

"And when are we to start, your excellency?"

"Well..." Anatole looked at his watch. "We'll start at once. Mind, Balagá! You'll get there in time? Eh?"

"That depends on our luck in starting, else why shouldn't we be there in time?" replied Balagá. "Didn't we get you to Tver in seven hours? I think you remember that, your excellency?"

"Do you know, one Christmas I drove from Tver," said Anatole, smilingly at the recollection and turning to Makárin who gazed rapturously at him with wide-open eyes. "Will you believe it, Makárka, it took one's breath away, the rate we flew. We came across a train of loaded sleighs and drove right over two of them. Eh?"

"Those were horses!" Balagá continued the tale. "That time I'd harnessed two young side horses with the bay in the shafts," he went on, turning to Dólokhov. "Will you believe it, Theodore Iványch, those animals flew forty miles? I couldn't hold them in, my hands grew numb in the sharp frost so that I threw down the reins—'Catch hold yourself, your excellency!' says I, and I just tumbled on the bottom of the sleigh and sprawled there. It wasn't a case of urging them on, there was no holding them in till we reached the place. The devils took us there in three hours! Only the near one died of it."

CHAPTER XVII

Anatole went out of the room and returned a few minutes later wearing a fur coat girt with a silver belt, and a sable cap jauntily set on one side and very becoming to his handsome face. Having looked in a mirror, and standing before Dólokhov in the same pose he had assumed before it, he lifted a glass of wine.

"Well, good-by, Theodore. Thank you for everything and farewell!" said Anatole. "Well, comrades and friends..." he considered for a moment "... of my youth, farewell!" he said, turning to Makárin and the others.

Though they were all going with him, Anatole evidently wished to make something touching and solemn out of this address to his comrades. He spoke slowly in a loud voice and throwing out his chest slightly swayed one leg.

"All take glasses; you too, Balagá. Well, comrades and friends of my youth, we've had our fling and lived and reveled. Eh? And now, when shall we meet again? I am going abroad. We have had a good time—now farewell, lads! To our health! Hurrah!..." he cried, and emptying his glass flung it on the floor.

"To your health!" said Balagá who also emptied his glass, and wiped his mouth with his handkerchief.

Makárin embraced Anatole with tears in his eyes.

"Ah, Prince, how sorry I am to part from you!"

"Let's go. Let's go!" cried Anatole.

Balagá was about to leave the room.

"No, stop!" said Anatole. "Shut the door; we have first to sit down. That's the way."

They shut the door and all sat down.

"Now, quick march, lads!" said Anatole, rising.

Joseph, his valet, handed him his sabretache and saber, and they all went out into the vestibule.

"And where's the fur cloak?" asked Dólokhov. "Hey, Ignátka! Go to MatrënaMatrévna and ask her for the sable cloak. I have heard what elopements are like," continued Dólokhov with a wink. "Why, she'll rush out more dead than alive just in the things she is wearing; if you delay at all there'll be tears and 'Papa' and 'Mamma,' and she's frozen in a minute and must go back—but you wrap the fur cloak round her first thing and carry her to the sleigh."

The valet brought a woman's fox-lined cloak.

"Fool, I told you the sable one! Hey, Matrëna, the sable!" he shouted so that his voice rang far through the rooms.

A handsome, slim, and pale-faced gypsy girl with glittering black eyes and curly blue-black hair, wearing a red shawl, ran out with a sable mantle on her arm.

"Here, I don't grudge it—take it!" she said, evidently afraid of her master and yet regretful of her cloak.

Dólokhov, without answering, took the cloak, threw it over Matrëna, and wrapped her up in it.

"That's the way," said Dólokhov, "and then so!" and he turned the collar up round her head, leaving only a little of the face uncovered. "And then so, do you see?" and he pushed Anatole's head forward to meet the gap left by the collar, through which Matrëna's brilliant smile was seen.

"Well, good-by, Matrëna," said Anatole, kissing her. "Ah, my revels here are over. Remember me to Stëshka. There, good-by! Good-by, Matrëna, wish me luck!"

"Well, Prince, may God give you great luck!" said Matrëna in her gypsy accent.

Two troykas were standing before the porch and two young drivers were holding the horses. Balagá took his seat in the front one and holding his elbows high arranged the reins deliberately. Anatole and Dólokhov got in with him. Makárin, Khvóstikov, and a valet seated themselves in the other sleigh.

"Well, are you ready?" asked Balagá.

"Go!" he cried, twisting the reins round his hands, and the troyka tore down the Nikítski Boulevard.

"Tproo! Get out of the way! Hi!... Tproo!..." The shouting of Balagá and of the sturdy young fellow seated on the box was all that could be heard. On the Arbát Square the troyka caught against a carriage; something cracked, shouts were heard, and the troyka flew along the Arbát Street.

After taking a turn along the Podnovínski Boulevard, Balagá began to rein in, and turning back drew up at the crossing of the old Konyúsheny Street.

The young fellow on the box jumped down to hold the horses and Anatole and Dólokhov went along the pavement. When they reached the gate Dólokhov whistled. The whistle was answered, and a maidservant ran out.

"Come into the courtyard or you'll be seen; she'll come out directly," said she.

Dólokhov stayed by the gate. Anatole followed the maid into the courtyard, turned the corner, and ran up into the porch.

He was met by Gabriel, MáryaDmítrievna's gigantic footman.

"Come to the mistress, please," said the footman in his deep bass, intercepting any retreat.

"To what Mistress? Who are you?" asked Anatole in a breathless whisper.

"Kindly step in, my orders are to bring you in."

"Kurágin! Come back!" shouted Dólokhov. "Betrayed! Back!"

Dólokhov, after Anatole entered, had remained at the wicket gate and was struggling with the yard porter who was trying to lock it. With a last desperate effort Dólokhov pushed the porter aside, and when Anatole ran back seized him by the arm, pulled him through the wicket, and ran back with him to the troyka.

CHAPTER XVIII

MáryaDmítrievna, having found Sónya weeping in the corridor, made her confess everything, and intercepting the note to Natásha she read it and went into Natásha's room with it in her hand. "You shameless good-for-nothing!" said she. "I won't hear a word."

Pushing back Natásha who looked at her with astonished but tearless eyes, she locked her in; and having given orders to the yard porter to admit the persons who would be coming that evening, but not to let them out again, and having told the footman to bring them up to her, she seated herself in the drawing room to await the abductors.

When Gabriel came to inform her that the men who had come had run away again, she rose frowning, and clasping her hands behind her paced through the rooms a long time considering what she should do. Toward midnight she went to Natásha's room fingering the key in her pocket. Sónya was sitting sobbing in the corridor. "MáryaDmítrievna, for God's sake let me in to her!" she pleaded, but MáryaDmítrievna unlocked the door and went in without giving her an answer.... "Disgusting, abominable... In my house... horrid girl, hussy! I'm only sorry for her father!" thought she, trying to restrain her wrath. "Hard as it may be, I'll tell them all to hold their tongues and will hide it from the count." She entered the room with resolute steps. Natásha lying on the sofa, her head hidden in her hands, and she did not stir. She was in just the same position in which MáryaDmítrievna had left her.

"A nice girl! Very nice!" said MáryaDmítrievna. "Arranging meetings with lovers in my house! It's no use pretending: you listen when I speak to you!" And MáryaDmítrievna touched her arm. "Listen when I speak! You've disgraced yourself like the lowest of hussies. I'd treat you differently, but I'm sorry for your father, so I will conceal it."

Natásha did not change her position, but her whole body heaved with noiseless, convulsive sobs which choked her. MáryaDmítrievna glanced round at Sónya and seated herself on the sofa beside Natásha.

"It's lucky for him that he escaped me; but I'll find him!" she said in her rough voice. "Do you hear what I am saying or not?" she added.

She put her large hand under Natásha's face and turned it toward her. Both MáryaDmítrievna and Sónya were amazed when they saw how Natásha looked. Her eyes were dry and glistening, her lips compressed, her cheeks sunken.

"Let me be!... What is it to me?... I shall die!" she muttered, wrenching herself from MáryaDmítrievna's hands with a vicious effort and sinking down again into her former position.

"Natalie!" said MáryaDmítrievna. "I wish for your good. Lie still, stay like that then, I won't touch you. But listen. I won't tell you how guilty you are. You know that yourself. But when your father comes back tomorrow what am I to tell him? Eh?"

AgainNatásha's body shook with sobs.

"Suppose he finds out, and your brother, and your betrothed?"

"I have no betrothed: I have refused him!" cried Natásha.

"That's all the same," continued MáryaDmítrievna. "If they hear of this, will they let it pass? He, your father, I know him... if he challenges him to a duel will that be all right? Eh?"

"Oh, let me be! Why have you interfered at all? Why? Why? Who asked you to?" shouted Natásha, raising herself on the sofa and looking malignantly at MáryaDmítrievna.

"But what did you want?" cried MáryaDmítrievna, growing angry again. "Were you kept under lock and key? Who hindered his coming to the house? Why carry you off as if you were some gypsy singing girl?... Well, if he had carried you off... do you think they wouldn't have found him? Your father, or brother, or your betrothed? And he's a scoundrel, a wretch—that's a fact!"

"He is better than any of you!" exclaimed Natásha getting up. "If you hadn't interfered... Oh, my God! What is it all? What is it? Sónya, why?... Go away!"

And she burst into sobs with the despairing vehemence with which people bewail disasters they feel they have themselves occasioned. MáryaDmítrievna was to speak again but Natásha cried out:

"Go away! Go away! You all hate and despise me!" and she threw herself back on the sofa.

MáryaDmítrievna went on admonishing her for some time, enjoining on her that it must all be kept from her father and assuring her that nobody would know anything about it if only Natásha herself would undertake to forget it all and not let anyone see that something had happened. Natásha did not reply, nor did she sob any longer, but she grew cold and had a shivering fit. MáryaDmítrievna put a pillow under her head, covered her with two quilts, and herself brought her some lime-flower water, but Natásha did not respond to her.

"Well, let her sleep," said MáryaDmítrievna as she went out of the room supposing Natásha to be asleep.

But Natásha was not asleep; with pale face and fixed wide-open eyes she looked straight before her. All that night she did not sleep or weep and did not speak to Sónya who got up and went to her several times.

Next day Count Rostóv returned from his estate near Moscow in time for lunch as he had promised. He was in very good spirits; the affair with the purchaser was going on satisfactorily, and there was nothing to keep him any longer in Moscow, away from the countess whom he missed. MáryaDmítrievna met him and told him that Natásha had been very unwell the day before and that they had sent for the doctor, but that she was better now. Natásha had not left her room that morning. With compressed and parched lips and dry fixed eyes, she sat at the window, uneasily watching the people who drove past and hurriedly glancing round at anyone who entered the room.

She was evidently expecting news of him and that he would come or would write to her.

When the count came to see her she turned anxiously round at the sound of a man's footstep, and then her face resumed its cold and malevolent expression. She did not even get up to greet him. "What is the matter with you, my angel? Are you ill?" asked the count.

After a moment's silence Natásha answered: "Yes, ill."

In reply to the count's anxious inquiries as to why she was so dejected and whether anything had happened to her betrothed, she assured him that nothing had happened and asked him not to worry. MáryaDmítrievna confirmed Natásha's assurances that nothing had happened. From the pretense of illness, from his daughter's distress, and by the embarrassed faces of Sónya and MáryaDmítrievna, the count saw clearly that something had gone wrong during his absence, but it was so terrible for him to think that anything disgraceful had happened to his beloved daughter, and he so prized his own cheerful tranquillity, that he avoided inquiries and tried to assure himself that nothing particularly had happened; and he was only dissatisfied that her indisposition delayed their return to the country.

CHAPTER XIX

From the day his wife arrived in Moscow Pierre had been intending to go away somewhere, so as not to be near her. Soon after the Rostóvs came to Moscow the effect Natásha had on him made him hasten to carry out his intention. He went to Tver to see Joseph Alexéevich's widow, who had long since promised to hand over to him some papers of her deceased husband's.

When he returned to Moscow Pierre was handed a letter from MáryaDmítrievna asking him to come and see her on a matter of great importance relating to Andrew Bolkónski and his betrothed. Pierre had been avoiding Natásha because it seemed to him that his feeling for her was stronger than a married man's should be for his friend's fiancée. Yet some fate constantly threw them together.

"What can have happened? And what can they want with me?" thought he as he dressed to go to MáryaDmítrievna's. "If only Prince Andrew would hurry up and come and marry her!" thought he on his way to the house.

On the Tverskóy Boulevard a familiar voice called to him.

"Pierre! Been back long?" someone shouted. Pierre raised his head. In a sleigh drawn by two gray trotting-horses that were bespattering the dashboard with snow, Anatole and his constant companion Makárin dashed past. Anatole was sitting upright in the classic pose of military dandies, the lower part of his face hidden by his beaver collar and his head slightly bent. His face was fresh and rosy, his white-plumed hat, tilted to one side, disclosed his curled and pomaded hair besprinkled with powdery snow.

"Yes, indeed, that's a true sage," thought Pierre. "He sees nothing beyond the pleasure of the moment, nothing troubles him and so he is always cheerful, satisfied, and serene. What wouldn't I give to be like him!" he thought enviously.

In MáryaDmítrievna's anteroom the footman who helped him off with his fur coat said that the mistress asked him to come to her bedroom.

When he opened the ballroom door Pierre saw Natásha sitting at the window, with a thin, pale, and spiteful face. She glanced round at him, frowned, and left the room with an expression of cold dignity.

"What has happened?" asked Pierre, entering MáryaDmítrievna's room.

"Fine doings!" answered Dmítrievna. "For fifty-eight years have I lived in this world and never known anything so disgraceful!"

And having put him on his honor not to repeat anything she told him, MáryaDmítrievna informed him that Natásha had refused Prince Andrew without her parents' knowledge and that the cause of this was Anatole Kurágin into whose society Pierre's wife had thrown her and with whom Natásha had tried to elope during her father's absence, in order to be married secretly.

Pierre raised his shoulders and listened open-mouthed to what was told him, scarcely able to believe his own ears. That Prince Andrew's deeply loved affianced wife—the same NatáshaRostóva who used to be so charming—should give up Bolkónski for that fool Anatole who was already secretly married (as Pierre knew), and should be so in love with him as to agree to run away with him, was something Pierre could not conceive and could not imagine.

He could not reconcile the charming impression he had of Natásha, whom he had known from a child, with this new conception of her baseness, folly, and cruelty. He thought of his wife. "They are all alike!" he said to himself, reflecting that he was not the only man unfortunate enough to be tied to a bad woman. But still he pitied Prince Andrew to the point of tears and sympathized with his wounded pride, and the more he pitied his friend the more did he think with contempt and even with disgust of that Natásha who had just passed him in the ballroom with such a look of cold dignity. He did not know that Natásha's soul was overflowing with despair, shame, and humiliation, and that it was not her fault that her face happened to assume an expression of calm dignity and severity.

"But how get married?" said Pierre, in answer to Márya Dmítrievna. "He could not marry—he is married!"

"Things get worse from hour to hour!" ejaculated Márya Dmítrievna. "A nice youth! What a scoundrel! And she's expecting him—expecting him since yesterday. She must be told! Then at least she won't go on expecting him."

After hearing the details of Anatole's marriage from Pierre, and giving vent to her anger against Anatole in words of abuse, Márya Dmítrievna told Pierre why she had sent for him. She was afraid that the count or Bolkónski, who might arrive at any moment, if they knew of this affair (which she hoped to hide from them) might challenge Anatole to a duel, and she therefore asked Pierre to tell his brother-in-law in her name to leave Moscow and not dare to let her set eyes on him again. Pierre—only now realizing the danger to the old count, Nicholas, and Prince Andrew—promised to do as she wished. Having briefly and exactly explained her wishes to him, she let him go to the drawing room.

"Mind, the count knows nothing. Behave as if you know nothing either," she said. "And I will go and tell her it is no use expecting him! And stay to dinner if you care to!" she called after Pierre.

Pierre met the old count, who seemed nervous and upset. That morning Natásha had told him that she had rejected Bolkónski.

"Troubles, troubles, my dear fellow!" he said to Pierre. "What troubles one has with these girls without their mother! I do so regret having come here.... I will be frank with you. Have you heard she has broken off her engagement without consulting anybody? It's true this engagement never was much to my liking. Of course he is an excellent man, but still, with his father's disapproval they wouldn't have been happy, and Natásha won't lack suitors. Still, it has been going on so long, and to take such a step without father's or mother's consent! And now she's ill, and God knows what! It's hard, Count, hard to manage daughters in their mother's absence...."

Pierre saw that the count was much upset and tried to change the subject, but the count returned to his troubles.

Sónya entered the room with an agitated face.

"Natásha is not quite well; she's in her room and would like to see you. MáryaDmítrievna is with her and she too asks you to come."

"Yes, you are a great friend of Bolkónski's, no doubt she wants to send him a message," said the count. "Oh dear! Oh dear! How happy it all was!"

And clutching the spare gray locks on his temples the count left the room.

When MáryaDmítrievna told Natásha that Anatole was married, Natásha did not wish to believe it and insisted on having it confirmed by Pierre himself. Sónya told Pierre this as she led him along the corridor to Natásha's room.

Natásha, pale and stern, was sitting beside MáryaDmítrievna, and her eyes, glittering feverishly, met Pierre with a questioning look the moment he entered. She did not smile or nod, but only gazed fixedly at him, and her look asked only one thing: was he a friend, or like the others an enemy in regard to Anatole? As for Pierre, he evidently did not exist for her.

"He knows all about it," said MáryaDmítrievna pointing to Pierre and addressing Natásha. "Let him tell you whether I have told the truth."

Natásha looked from one to the other as a hunted and wounded animal looks at the approaching dogs and sportsmen.

"NatályaIlyníchna," Pierre began, dropping his eyes with a feeling of pity for her and loathing for the thing he had to do, "whether it is true or not should make no difference to you, because..."

"Then it is not true that he's married!"

"Yes, it is true."

"Has he been married long?" she asked. "On your honor?..."

Pierre gave his word of honor.

"Is he still here?" she asked, quickly.

"Yes, I have just seen him."

She was evidently unable to speak and made a sign with her hands that they should leave her alone.

CHAPTER XX

Pierre did not stay for dinner, but left the room and went away at once. He drove through the town seeking Anatole Kurágin, at the thought of whom now the blood rushed to his heart and he felt a difficulty in breathing. He was not at the ice hills, nor at the gypsies', nor at Komoneno's. Pierre drove to the Club. In the Club all was going on as usual. The members who were assembling for dinner were sitting about in groups; they greeted Pierre and spoke of the town news. The footman having greeted him, knowing his habits and his acquaintances, told him there was a place left for him in the small dining room and that Prince Michael Zakhárych was in the library, but Paul Timoféevich had not yet arrived. One of Pierre's acquaintances, while they were talking about the weather, asked if he had heard of Kurágin's abduction of Rostóva which was talked of in the town, and was it true? Pierre laughed and said it was nonsense for he had just come from the Rostóvs'. He asked everyone about Anatole. One man told him he had not come yet, and another that he was coming to dinner. Pierre felt it strange to see this calm, indifferent crowd of people unaware of what was going on in his soul. He paced through the ballroom, waited till everyone had come, and as Anatole had not turned up did not stay for dinner but drove home.

Anatole, for whom Pierre was looking, dined that day with Dólokhov, consulting him as to how to remedy this unfortunate affair. It seemed to him essential to see Natásha. In the evening he drove to his sister's to discuss with her how to arrange a meeting. When Pierre returned home after vainly hunting all over Moscow, his valet informed him that Prince Anatole was with the countess. The countess' drawing room was full of guests.

Pierre without greeting his wife whom he had not seen since his return—at that moment she was more repulsive to him than ever—entered the drawing room and seeing Anatole went up to him.

"Ah, Pierre," said the countess going up to her husband. "You don't know what a plight our Anatole..."

She stopped, seeing in the forward thrust of her husband's head, in his glowing eyes and his resolute gait, the terrible indications of that rage and strength which she knew and had herself experienced after his duel with Dólokhov.

"Where you are, there is vice and evil!" said Pierre to his wife. "Anatole, come with me! I must speak to you," he added in French.

Anatole glanced round at his sister and rose submissively, ready to follow Pierre. Pierre, taking him by the arm, pulled him toward himself and was leading him from the room.

"If you allow yourself in my drawing room..." whispered Hélène, but Pierre did not reply and went out of the room.

Anatole followed him with his usual jaunty step but his face betrayed anxiety.

Having entered his study Pierre closed the door and addressed Anatole without looking at him.

"You promised Countess Rostóva to marry her and were about to elope with her, is that so?"

"*Mon cher,*" answered Anatole (their whole conversation was in French), "I don't consider myself bound to answer questions put to me in that tone."

Pierre's face, already pale, became distorted by fury. He seized Anatole by the collar of his uniform with his big hand and shook him from side to side till Anatole's face showed a sufficient degree of terror.

"When I tell you that I must talk to you!..." repeated Pierre.

"Come now, this is stupid. What?" said Anatole, fingering a button of his collar that had been wrenched loose with a bit of the cloth.

"You're a scoundrel and a blackguard, and I don't know what deprives me from the pleasure of smashing your head with this!" said Pierre, expressing himself so artificially because he was talking French.

He took a heavy paperweight and lifted it threateningly, but at once put it back in its place.

"Did you promise to marry her?"

"I... I didn't think of it. I never promised, because..."

Pierre interrupted him.

"Have you any letters of hers? Any letters?" he said, moving toward Anatole.

Anatole glanced at him and immediately thrust his hand into his pocket and drew out his pocketbook.

Pierre took the letter Anatole handed him and, pushing aside a table that stood in his way, threw himself on the sofa.

"I shan't be violent, don't be afraid!" said Pierre in answer to a frightened gesture of Anatole's. "First, the letters," said he, as if repeating a lesson to himself. "Secondly," he continued after a short pause, again rising and again pacing the room, "tomorrow you must get out of Moscow."

"But how can I?..."

"Thirdly," Pierre continued without listening to him, "you must never breathe a word of what has passed between you and Countess Rostóva. I know I can't prevent your doing so, but if you have a spark of conscience..." Pierre paced the room several times in silence.

Anatole sat at a table frowning and biting his lips.

"After all, you must understand that besides your pleasure there is such a thing as other people's happiness and peace, and that you are ruining a whole life for the sake of amusing yourself! Amuse yourself with women like my wife—with them you are within your rights, for they know what you want of them. They are armed against you by the same experience of debauchery; but to promise a *maid* to marry her... to deceive, to kidnap.... Don't you understand that it is as mean as beating an old man or a child?..."

Pierre paused and looked at Anatole no longer with an angry but with a questioning look.

"I don't know about that, eh?" said Anatole, growing more confident as Pierre mastered his wrath. "I don't know that and don't want to," he said, not looking at Pierre and with a slight tremor of his lower jaw, "but you have used such words to me—'mean' and so on—which as a man of honor I can't allow anyone to use."

Pierre glanced at him with amazement, unable to understand what he wanted.

"Though it was tête-à-tête," Anatole continued, "still I can't..."

"Is it satisfaction you want?" said Pierre ironically.

"You could at least take back your words. What? If you want me to do as you wish, eh?"

"I take them back, I take them back!" said Pierre, "and I ask you to forgive me." Pierre involuntarily glanced at the loose button. "And if you require money for your journey..."

Anatole smiled. The expression of that base and cringing smile, which Pierre knew so well in his wife, revolted him.

"Oh, vile and heartless brood!" he exclaimed, and left the room.

Next day Anatole left for Petersburg.

CHAPTER XXI

Pierre drove to MáryaDmítrievna's to tell her of the fulfillment of her wish that Kurágin should be banished from Moscow. The whole house was in a state of alarm and commotion. Natásha was very ill, having, as MáryaDmítrievna told him in secret, poisoned herself the night after she had been told that Anatole was married, with some arsenic she had stealthily procured. After swallowing a little she had been so frightened that she woke Sónya and told her what she had done. The necessary antidotes had been administered in time and she was now out of danger, though still so weak that it was out of the question to move her to the country, and so the countess had been sent for. Pierre saw the distracted count, and Sónya, who had a tear-stained face, but he could not see Natásha.

Pierre dined at the club that day and heard on all sides gossip about the attempted abduction of Rostóva. He resolutely denied these rumors, assuring everyone that nothing had happened except that his brother-in-law had proposed to her and been refused. It seemed to Pierre that it was his duty to conceal the whole affair and re-establish Natásha's reputation.

He was awaiting Prince Andrew's return with dread and went every day to the old prince's for news of him.

Old Prince Bolkónski heard all the rumors current in the town from Mademoiselle Bourienne and had read the note to Princess Mary in which Natásha had broken off her engagement. He seemed in better spirits than usual and awaited his son with great impatience.

Some days after Anatole's departure Pierre received a note from Prince Andrew, informing him of his arrival and asking him to come to see him.

As soon as he reached Moscow, Prince Andrew had received from his father Natásha's note to Princess Mary breaking off her engagement (Mademoiselle Bourienne had purloined it from Princess Mary and given it to the old prince), and he heard from him the story of Natásha's elopement, with additions.

Prince Andrew had arrived in the evening and Pierre came to see him next morning. Pierre expected to find Prince Andrew in almost the same state as Natásha and was therefore surprised on entering the drawing room to hear him in the study talking in a loud animated voice about some intrigue going on in Petersburg. The old prince's voice and another now and then interrupted him. Princess Mary came out to meet Pierre. She sighed, looking toward the door of the room where Prince Andrew was, evidently intending to express her sympathy with his sorrow, but Pierre saw by her face that she was glad both at what had happened and at the way her brother had taken the news of Natásha's faithlessness.

"He says he expected it," she remarked. "I know his pride will not let him express his feelings, but still he has taken it better, far better, than I expected. Evidently it had to be...."

"But is it possible that all is really ended?" asked Pierre.

Princess Mary looked at him with astonishment. She did not understand how he could ask such a question. Pierre went into the study. Prince Andrew, greatly changed and plainly in better health, but with a fresh horizontal wrinkle between his brows, stood in civilian dress facing his father and Prince Meshchérski, warmly disputing and vigorously gesticulating. The conversation was about Speránski—the news of whose sudden exile and alleged treachery had just reached Moscow.

"Now he is censured and accused by all who were enthusiastic about him a month ago," Prince Andrew was saying, "and by those who were unable to understand his aims. To judge a man who is in disfavor and to throw on him all the blame of other men's mistakes is very easy, but I maintain that if anything good has been accomplished in this reign it was done by him, by him alone."

He paused at the sight of Pierre. His face quivered and immediately assumed a vindictive expression.

"Posterity will do him justice," he concluded, and at once turned to Pierre.

"Well, how are you? Still getting stouter?" he said with animation, but the new wrinkle on his forehead deepened. "Yes, I am well," he said in answer to Pierre's question, and smiled.

To Pierre that smile said plainly: "I am well, but my health is now of no use to anyone."

After a few words to Pierre about the awful roads from the Polish frontier, about people he had met in Switzerland who knew Pierre, and about M. Dessalles, whom he had brought from abroad to be his son's tutor, Prince Andrew again joined warmly in the conversation about Speránski which was still going on between the two old men.

"If there were treason, or proofs of secret relations with Napoleon, they would have been made public," he said with warmth and haste. "I do not, and never did, like Speránski personally, but I like justice!"

Pierre now recognized in his friend a need with which he was only too familiar, to get excited and to have arguments about extraneous matters in order to stifle thoughts that were too oppressive and too intimate. When Prince Meshchérski had left, Prince Andrew took Pierre's arm and asked him into the room that had been assigned him. A bed had been made up there, and some open portmanteaus and trunks stood about. Prince Andrew went to one and took out a small casket, from which he drew a packet wrapped in paper. He did it all silently and very quickly. He stood up and coughed. His face was gloomy and his lips compressed.

"Forgive me for troubling you...."

Pierre saw that Prince Andrew was going to speak of Natásha, and his broad face expressed pity and sympathy. This expression irritated Prince Andrew, and in a determined, ringing, and unpleasant tone he continued:

"I have received a refusal from Countess Rostóva and have heard reports of your brother-in-law having sought her hand, or something of that kind. Is that true?"

"Both true and untrue," Pierre began; but Prince Andrew interrupted him.

"Here are her letters and her portrait," said he.

He took the packet from the table and handed it to Pierre.

"Give this to the countess... if you see her."

"She is very ill," said Pierre.

"Then she is here still?" said Prince Andrew. "And Prince Kurágin?" he added quickly.

"He left long ago. She has been at death's door."

"I much regret her illness," said Prince Andrew; and he smiled like his father, coldly, maliciously, and unpleasantly.

"So Monsieur Kurágin has not honored Countess Rostóva with his hand?" said Prince Andrew, and he snorted several times.

"He could not marry, for he was married already," said Pierre.

Prince Andrew laughed disagreeably, again reminding one of his father.

"And where is your brother-in-law now, if I may ask?" he said.

"He has gone to Peters... But I don't know," said Pierre.

"Well, it doesn't matter," said Prince Andrew. "Tell Countess Rostóva that she was and is perfectly free and that I wish her all that is good."

Pierre took the packet. Prince Andrew, as if trying to remember whether he had something more to say, or waiting to see if Pierre would say anything, looked fixedly at him.

"I say, do you remember our discussion in Petersburg?" asked Pierre, "about..."

"Yes," returned Prince Andrew hastily. "I said that a fallen woman should be forgiven, but I didn't say I could forgive her. I can't."

"But can this be compared...?" said Pierre.

Prince Andrew interrupted him and cried sharply: "Yes, ask her hand again, be magnanimous, and so on?... Yes, that would be very noble, but I am unable to follow in that gentleman's footsteps. If you wish to be my friend never speak to me of that... of all that! Well, good-by. So you'll give her the packet?"

Pierre left the room and went to the old prince and Princess Mary.

The old man seemed livelier than usual. Princess Mary was the same as always, but beneath her sympathy for her brother, Pierre noticed her satisfaction that the engagement had been broken off. Looking at them Pierre realized what contempt and animosity they all felt for the Rostóvs, and that it was impossible in their presence even to mention the name of her who could give up Prince Andrew for anyone else.

At dinner the talk turned on the war, the approach of which was becoming evident. Prince Andrew talked incessantly, arguing now with his father, now with the Swiss tutor Dessalles, and showing an unnatural animation, the cause of which Pierre so well understood.

CHAPTER XXII

That same evening Pierre went to the Rostóvs' to fulfill the commission entrusted to him. Natásha was in bed, the count at the club, and Pierre, after giving the letters to Sónya, went to MáryaDmítrievna who was interested to know how Prince Andrew had taken the news. Ten minutes later Sónya came to MáryaDmítrievna.

"Natásha insists on seeing Count Peter Kirílovich," said she.

"But how? Are we to take him up to her? The room there has not been tidied up."

"No, she has dressed and gone into the drawing room," said Sónya.

MáryaDmítrievna only shrugged her shoulders.

"When will her mother come? She has worried me to death! Now mind, don't tell her everything!" said she to Pierre. "One hasn't the heart to scold her, she is so much to be pitied, so much to be pitied."

Natásha was standing in the middle of the drawing room, emaciated, with a pale set face, but not at all shamefaced as Pierre expected to find her. When he appeared at the door she grew flurried, evidently undecided whether to go to meet him or to wait till he came up.

Pierre hastened to her. He thought she would give him her hand as usual; but she, stepping up to him, stopped, breathing heavily, her arms hanging lifelessly just in the pose she used to stand in when she went to the middle of the ballroom to sing, but with quite a different expression of face.

"Peter Kirílovich," she began rapidly, "Prince Bolkónski was your friend—is your friend," she corrected herself. (It seemed to her that everything that had once been must now be different.) "He told me once to apply to you..."

Pierre sniffed as he looked at her, but did not speak. Till then he had reproached her in his heart and tried to despise her, but he now felt so sorry for her that there was no room in his soul for reproach.

"He is here now: tell him... to for... forgive me!" She stopped and breathed still more quickly, but did not shed tears.

"Yes... I will tell him," answered Pierre; "but..."

He did not know what to say.

Natásha was evidently dismayed at the thought of what he might think she had meant.

"No, I know all is over," she said hurriedly. "No, that can never be. I'm only tormented by the wrong I have done him. Tell him only that I beg him to forgive, forgive, forgive me for everything...."

She trembled all over and sat down on a chair.

A sense of pity he had never before known overflowed Pierre's heart.

"I will tell him, I will tell him everything once more," said Pierre. "But... I should like to know one thing...."

"Know what?" Natásha's eyes asked.

"I should like to know, did you love..." Pierre did not know how to refer to Anatole and flushed at the thought of him—"did you love that bad man?"

"Don't call him bad!" said Natásha. "But I don't know, don't know at all...."

She began to cry and a still greater sense of pity, tenderness, and love welled up in Pierre. He felt the tears trickle under his spectacles and hoped they would not be noticed.

"We won't speak of it any more, my dear," said Pierre, and his gentle, cordial tone suddenly seemed very strange to Natásha.

"We won't speak of it, my dear—I'll tell him everything; but one thing I beg of you, consider me your friend and if you want help, advice, or simply to open your heart to someone—not now, but when your mind is clearer—think of me!" He took her hand and kissed it. "I shall be happy if it's in my power..."

Pierre grew confused.

"Don't speak to me like that. I am not worth it!" exclaimed Natásha and turned to leave the room, but Pierre held her hand.

He knew he had something more to say to her. But when he said it he was amazed at his own words.

"Stop, stop! You have your whole life before you," said he to her.

"Before me? No! All is over for me," she replied with shame and self-abasement.

"All over?" he repeated. "If I were not myself, but the handsomest, cleverest, and best man in the world, and were free, I would this moment ask on my knees for your hand and your love!"

For the first time for many days Natásha wept tears of gratitude and tenderness, and glancing at Pierre she went out of the room.

Pierre too when she had gone almost ran into the anteroom, restraining tears of tenderness and joy that choked him, and without finding the sleeves of his fur cloak threw it on and got into his sleigh.

"Where to now, your excellency?" asked the coachman.

"Where to?" Pierre asked himself. "Where can I go now? Surely not to the Club or to pay calls?" All men seemed so pitiful, so poor, in comparison with this feeling of tenderness and love he experienced: in comparison with that softened, grateful, last look she had given him through her tears.

"Home!" said Pierre, and despite twenty-two degrees of frost Fahrenheit he threw open the bearskin cloak from his broad chest and inhaled the air with joy.

It was clear and frosty. Above the dirty, ill-lit streets, above the black roofs, stretched the dark starry sky. Only looking up at the sky did Pierre cease to feel how sordid and humiliating were all mundane things compared with the heights to which his soul had just been raised. At the entrance to the Arbát Square an immense expanse of dark starry sky presented itself to his eyes. Almost in the center of it, above the Prechístenka Boulevard, surrounded and sprinkled on all sides by stars but distinguished from them all by its nearness to the earth, its white light, and its long uplifted tail, shone the enormous and brilliant comet of 1812—the comet which was said to portend all kinds of woes and the end of the world. In Pierre, however, that comet with its long luminous tail aroused no feeling of fear. On the contrary he gazed joyfully, his eyes moist with tears, at this bright comet which, having traveled in its orbit with inconceivable velocity through immeasurable space, seemed suddenly—like an arrow piercing the earth—to remain fixed in a chosen spot, vigorously holding its tail erect, shining and displaying its white light amid countless other scintillating stars. It seemed to Pierre that this comet fully responded to what was passing in his own softened and uplifted soul, now blossoming into a new life.